What had almost happened between her and Garrett yesterday? Had it been an almost kiss? If so, she had pulled away from it, hadn't she?

Gwen gave herself a mental shake and told herself to slow down. She didn't get infatuated with men, she reminded herself. She was picky, and a rugged face with a good body might turn her head, but it didn't stay turned. She wanted substance.

You thought you had substance with Mark, a little voice reminded her.

She'd been so wrong about that. She'd been so wrong about a lot of things. But she was working on fixing them.

And then she opened the door to Garrett—and common sense flew out the proverbial window. She was attracted to him, plain and simple. She would have to watch every step she made....

Dear Reader,

I can't imagine going through life without true friends. My best friend from grade school and I have kept in touch all these years. As I remember high school, I picture the group of girls I had lunch with, talked about boys with and studied with. We supported each other's dreams. My college roommate and I have celebrated New Year's Eve together for the past thirty years. Then there's my husband: my very best friend. He believes he knows what I'm thinking and usually he does. But once in a while, I still surprise him!

In *The Baby Trail,* Gwen has relied on her friends all her life. When Garrett enters her world, she realizes she needs her friends as much as ever. Yet she discovers her attraction and deepening love for Garrett lead to a soul-mate friendship she never expected to find.

I wish my readers friendships of all kinds that last a lifetime.

All my best,

Karen Rose Smith

THE BABY TRAIL

KAREN ROSE SMITH

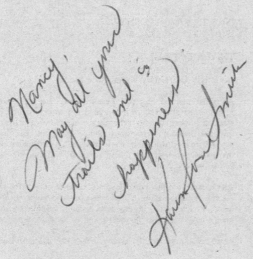

Silhouette®

SPECIAL EDITION®

Published by Silhouette Books

America's Publisher of Contemporary Romance

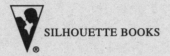 **SILHOUETTE BOOKS**

ISBN-13: 978-0-373-24767-7
ISBN-10:   0-373-24767-2

THE BABY TRAIL

Copyright © 2006 by Karen Rose Smith

Visit Silhouette Books at www.eHarlequin.com

Printed in U.S.A.

KAREN ROSE SMITH

read Zane Grey when she was in grade school and loved his books. She also had a crush on Roy Rogers and especially his palomino, Trigger! Around horses as a child, she found them fascinating and intuitive. This series of books set in Wyoming sprang from childhood wishes and adult dreams. When an acquaintance adopted two of the wild mustangs from the western rangelands and invited Karen to visit them, plotlines weren't far behind. For more background on the books in the series, stop by Karen's Web site at www.karenrosesmith.com or write to her at P.O. Box 1545, Hanover, PA 17331.

In loving memory of my mom and dad—
Romaine Arcuri Cacciola and Angelo Jacob Cacciola.
I'm so grateful for your love and care as parents.
I miss you.

To my husband, Steve—
it was a trip of a lifetime I could only have taken and
appreciated with you. I'll never forget our first sighting of
the wild mustangs in the Big Horns.

To my son, Ken—May your dreams always run free.

Thanks to my cousin Paul Arcuri, pilot and
my advisor on all things aeronautic.

For more information about wild mustangs,
visit www.wildhorsepreservation.com. For adoption
information go to www.wildhorseandburro.blm.gov.

Chapter One

A baby's cry tore through Gwen Langworthy's small house. It only took a moment for her to realize the sound was coming from her sunroom!

Dusk had fallen and shadows were thick in the ranch-style house as she raced from the kitchen through the living room. As an obstetrical nurse practitioner, she was well aware of babies' cries. They always ripped a corner of her heart. She longed to have a baby of her own.

The first cry whimpered into a second as she reached for the ceramic light on the wicker table inside the sunroom and saw a blue plastic bin sitting just inside her sliding glass doors. Rushing to it, she hunkered down. An infant with sparkling dark eyes, who couldn't be more than a day or two old, stared up at her. Layers of newspaper lined the inside of the bin, but the baby was nestled in a pink blanket. A torn sheet of notebook paper lay at her feet with "Amy" written in block letters.

It was a little girl!

After pushing her auburn curls behind her ears, Gwen reflexively scooped up the child and cuddled her in her arms. Dreams of happily-ever-after and having the family she'd always wanted had evaporated like smoke after Mark had left her waiting with her dad at the white runner that was supposed to lead her to commitment and everlasting bonds. His abandonment still hurt, and she didn't think she could ever trust a man again.

"So your name is Amy," she murmured, the nurse in her already taking in every detail about the child's physical condition. Her maternal instincts led her to notice the baby's little sweater and hat fashioned of soft fuzzy yarn in variegated white, yellow and aqua. The set looked as if it had been hand-knitted. Someone had cared about this child.

And then abandoned her?

Gwen knew all about that kind of abandonment, too.

Stepping toward the glass doors, Gwen slid one open. The evening's breeze swept in as she stared deep into her yard. A street ran to the back of it. Was that a car engine she heard coughing, then starting up? She couldn't see between the shadowed trees. Fall in Wyoming was closing in.

Little Amy wiggled in her arms, screwed up her face and let out another wail.

Hugging Amy close, Gwen went to the phone to call one of her best friends, who was a social worker. But she already knew what Shaye would advise her to do: call the sheriff.

Thinking about a sheriff who was more focused on his impending retirement than serving the residents of Wild Horse Junction, she decided if he didn't make progress at finding Amy's mother within a week, she'd take matters into her own hands.

She wouldn't let this child go through life not knowing where she came from…never knowing why her mother hadn't loved her enough to keep her.

"Mr. Maxwell," Gwen called above the loud banging that made her cringe.

The noise suddenly ceased. In an instant Garrett Maxwell, if that's who he was, went from hammering a floorboard to a standing defensive stance, his hammer held almost like a weapon. With dark brown hair, he was tall, over six feet, broad-shouldered in a black T-shirt, slim-hipped in well-worn blue jeans. His presence totally overwhelmed the small backyard shed and in the dim light, his gray eyes targeted and held her at the threshold.

"Can I help you?" His voice was filled with icy calm and she instantly felt like an intruder.

"I hope so," she answered fervently and saw the interest in his eyes.

Garrett Maxwell had the reputation for being a recluse, working from his log house in the foothills of Wyoming's Painted Peaks. She'd known about his credentials because of an article she'd read in the *Wild Horse Wrangler* a few months ago—he had helped locate a missing child in Colorado. Before driving up here, she'd searched for information about him on the Internet and found several articles noting how he helped search-and-rescue teams with lost children and aided in child-kidnapping cases.

When he didn't move a muscle, when his strong jaw remained set, when he didn't invite her to tell him her reason for coming, she plunged in, anyway.

"Are you Garrett Maxwell?"

"Who wants to know?"

Although she wasn't sure if it was wise, she took a couple of steps forward.

His gaze raked over her lime-green blouse and khaki slacks. Even though this perusal of her took about a second, she felt as if he'd noticed every detail from the number of curls in her shoulder-length hair to her brown loafers.

Gwen was feeling as though she was poking her hand into a lethal animal's cage but she extended it anyway. "My name's Gwen Langworthy."

He didn't shake her hand; however, his grip loosened on the hammer and he dropped it onto the seat of the mower. "How can I help you?"

It had been five days since little Amy had been left in her sunroom. Gwen still didn't know who had left her or why, but she did know the sheriff hadn't gotten anywhere on identifying the infant. Impatient with him, she was now taking matters into her own hands. She didn't want Amy going through life never knowing where she came from. Gwen had carried *that* burden on her own shoulders—she'd been abandoned in a church when she was only two. She knew all the self-doubt that went with not knowing her birth parents…the introspective questions no one could answer.

Quickly stuffing both hands into her pockets, she wondered why her stomach fluttered when she looked at the former FBI agent. Was she afraid of him? No. She was mesmerized by him. He reeked sensuality, power….

Grabbing on to her reason for coming, she explained, "I know you can find people. I need you to find someone for me."

"I don't find *people*."

"You find *children*."

Now he finally looked interested. "Did you lose a child?"

Was she imagining it or had his voice turned almost gentle? "No I didn't, but I need to find a child's mother."

The gruffness returned. "I'm not FBI, anymore."

She wasn't about to give up without a fight. This man was good at what he did. He was the expert she needed and she *would* convince him that Amy needed him. "I know that. You have a security consulting business now. But you *were* an FBI agent and I need your help. Someone left a baby at my back door. I won't let that little girl grow up never knowing who her birth parents were. And I know that each day that goes by the trail gets colder."

His right eyebrow quirked slightly as if she'd finally made a dent in the shield he'd wrapped around himself. "Why do you care so much?"

She didn't hesitate. "Because I was adopted and

never knew who my birth parents were. And neither did anyone else."

The September wind whistled through the lodgepole pines and Russian olive trees, then gusted through the door of the shed, sending leaves scattering.

After a few moments of thoughtful consideration, the ex-FBI agent said, "Let's go to the house." He motioned outside at the granite stepping stones that led to his back deck.

Although Gwen's surroundings might have taken her attention any other time—there was something primitively beautiful about the property—she couldn't keep her gaze from Garrett Maxwell's broad back or the way he fit his jeans. Something about him, maybe that innate sensuality she'd sensed, stirred a deep womanlike corner inside of her. It was a terrifically odd, exciting, confusing sensation.

They passed a gazebolike structure on the deck. At the back door, he stopped and stepped aside to let her precede him. He was scowling and she couldn't imagine why.

Inside his kitchen, the pleasing knotty pine atmosphere surrounded her immediately. A small round wooden table and chairs stood in a breakfast nook with windows overlooking the back of the property.

When she turned her gaze back to him, he was watching her. A free-fall sensation made her catch her breath as she looked into his very gray eyes.

He broke eye contact and motioned to the counter. "Coffee?" he asked as if he was aware he had to be civil to a guest.

Her mouth had gone dry and she needed something

to wet her tongue if she was going to tell her story. She nodded.

Pouring coffee into two large mugs, he motioned to the counter. "I only have powdered creamer. Sugar's in the canister beside it."

When Gwen opened the stoneware canister, she found her hands were shaking. She'd never found herself in quite this situation before—highly attracted to a stranger and alone with him in his secluded house.

The lid on the canister flipped and clattered onto the counter.

Garrett Maxwell picked it up, held it and pinned her with his stormy eyes. "There's nothing to be nervous about. I'll listen, but I might not be able to help."

"I'm not nervous," she returned defensively. She was used to handling everything that came her way—her parents' divorce, her dad's drinking, her attempt at intervention to make Russ Langworthy finally face reality.

"Then you're doing a good imitation. How much sugar?"

She blinked, forgetting why she was standing at his counter.

"In your coffee." He nodded toward the mug he'd poured for her.

"A teaspoon." Her voice came out thready.

When he reached around her, his long arm brushed her hip. She swallowed hard, frozen for the moment.

Opening the drawer beside her, he pulled out a spoon and handed it to her. After he closed the drawer and leaned away again, she finally released her breath, took the utensil without allowing her fingers to brush his and spooned sugar from the cannister. He was watching her and she didn't like the idea that he was trying to "read" her.

With a half smile, he took a pack of creamer from a jelly jar. "One or two?"

"One is fine."

This time when he handed it to her, their fingers did brush. The expression on his face didn't change, but she glimpsed a sparklike flicker in his eyes. Could he be attracted to her, too?

So what if he was. She'd come to enlist his help, not to step into another romantic quagmire.

Maxwell let her precede him to the table in the breakfast nook. When she was seated, he dropped into a ladderback chair across from her, took a few sips of his coffee and assessed her over its rim. "So…tell me what this is about."

After her own sip of coffee, she told him how she'd found baby Amy in her sunroom.

"And you didn't hear anyone outside?" he asked.

"No. I just heard the baby cry. After I found her, I looked out and thought I heard a car start up. But it was getting dark and I couldn't see."

"A smooth start or a rough start?" he asked.

"I don't know."

"Yes, you do. Think about it."

As she tried to take herself back to that evening, she remembered holding Amy in her arms and attempting to search through the dusk. She'd heard a chug-chug, then a va-room, before the vehicle sped away. "It wasn't a smooth start. There was chugging first."

Maxwell seemed to make a mental note of that. "You

said your friend, Shaye Malloy, who is a social worker, arrived. And then the sheriff came. What did he do with the note with the baby's name on it?"

"He looked at it, then slipped it into his pocket."

Garrett Maxwell shook his head and his jaw tightened. Then he asked her, "What was the baby wearing?"

The former agent's face had lines around his eyes and mouth. Gwen guessed he was nearing forty. Had he left the FBI because the job had taken its toll? His face was so interesting, so ruggedly angular, she could look at him all day.

But that wasn't why she was here.

"Amy was nestled in a blanket, but she had on this cute little sweater and hat and one of those one-piece terry playsuits...in yellow."

"Why did you call the social worker? Wouldn't the sheriff have done that?"

"Shaye and I have been friends a long time. I wasn't about to let Amy out of my hands without knowing someone who cared was looking after her." Before Shaye and the sheriff had arrived, Gwen had cuddled Amy, rocked her, crooned to her, and it had been very difficult to let Shaye take her.

When Garrett Maxwell's penetrating gaze focused on her, Gwen felt turned inside out.

"Where is she now?" he asked.

"In the hospital's nursery."

He leaned back in his chair and it creaked. "Does she *need* to be in the hospital?"

Suddenly Gwen decided she wouldn't want to be interrogated by this man. He was methodical and thorough. "The doctor examined her and found she was jaundiced. She's over that, but now they're trying to find a family to take her. I would have liked to, but—"

"What?" Garrett asked, his gaze probing.

Gwen felt she was too close to him, though the distance of the table separated them. "I have to work, and I'd have to find someone to babysit. Besides that, I'm a firm believer a child should ideally have two parents—two parents who are going to love her forever. And it's just me, so I couldn't give her that. Shaye says they can easily find a couple who will…if we don't find the mother."

Garrett's gaze closely appraised her again until she felt like shifting in her chair. Finally he commented, "If you *do* find the mother, the child will be taken away from her, anyway."

"Maybe. But Shaye says it depends on the circumstances. It's not like she abandoned her in a dumpster or in a cold alley. I'm racking my brain to figure out who might have known me and why they would have left the baby with me. I've met a lot of unwed mothers."

"How so?" He took a long swallow of coffee.

"I'm a nurse practitioner, and I specialize in obstetrics. I help set up programs for unwed mothers."

"In Wild Horse Junction?"

"All over the state."

After he seemed to absorb that information, he stood. "There's not much here to go on."

Gwen wasn't ready for this meeting with him to be over. Because of Amy. Because… Simply because. "I read you're good at what you do. I know you can find her."

"Miss Langworthy—"

"Gwen," she corrected him, forestalling him, not wanting him to tell her he wouldn't take the case. "I'll pay you," she hurried on. "I'll pay you somehow, whatever you charge. This little girl deserves to know who her mother is. She deserves to know why her mother left her with me. If she goes through life always wondering—" Gwen stopped abruptly.

Rounding the table, Garrett Maxwell stood close by her side. "What will that do to her?" His eyes were suddenly compassionate.

"It will make her unsure of who she is and where she came from. And who she might become," Gwen murmured, unwilling to reveal too much.

"We're not talking about Baby Amy now, are we?" The question was rhetorical, and he was trying to make a point.

Looking him squarely in the eyes, Gwen answered, "We're talking about any child who doesn't know his or her roots."

Neither of them looked away. The moment palpitated with Gwen's passion for the search along with man-woman awareness.

Finally Gwen asked, "Will you help me find Amy's mother?" That was the bottom line for her and all that mattered.

"I usually search for children, not parents."

There was steel in his tone, and she had the feeling he didn't change his mind once he made a decision.

"Can you make an exception?"

Time ticked by in interminable seconds until he assured her, "I'll think about it and get back to you."

Her stomach sank and she stood. Pulling a business card from her pocket, she laid it on the table. "When?" she asked, aware of the we'll-get-back-to-you line and professionals who never did.

"You need an answer soon because you're going to find a P.I. to do this if I won't?" he guessed.

"Exactly. I don't give up easily, Mr. Maxwell. And I don't have much time."

After a few more beats of studying her, he muttered, "I guess you don't. I'll call you tomorrow evening with my answer."

They were close enough to touch…close enough to breathe the same breakfast-nook air…close enough that his scent—male mixed with outdoors—was a potent fantasy generator. But Gwen didn't indulge in fantasies anymore—not since her last vestige of trust in men had been crushed.

Garrett Maxwell's words were an obvious dismissal. When he motioned toward the front of the house and said, "I'll walk you out," she went that way, illogically curious about how this enigmatic man lived.

She didn't have time to take in every nuance, but she did spot the hall that must have led to downstairs bedrooms, the loft with a Native American blanket hanging over the railing, the stone fireplace.

At his front door now, she extended her hand to him again. "It was good to meet you, Mr. Maxwell."

This time he took her hand and when palm met palm, she felt a jolt of attraction that was so electric her breath caught. If she had to say how long their hands were clasped, there was no way she could. Ten seconds…twenty minutes…a half hour. There was no time, only the deep gray of Garrett Maxwell's eyes, the heat of his skin against hers. It was a moment she'd remember for a long time to come.

Suddenly he dropped his hand, and she turned to the cooler outside air so he wouldn't see the heat burning her cheeks. She didn't know whether to hope Garrett Maxwell took the case or didn't. Yet she knew if he did, he'd find Amy's mother.

Chapter Two

Garrett stared through the glass window of the hospital nursery at Baby Amy, and a lead stone turned in his gut. If everything had gone as planned, he would have been the father of a five-year-old right now. But everything hadn't gone as planned. Cheryl had miscarried and blamed him. His divorce had made him rethink his work and his life and that's how he'd ended up back in Wild Horse Junction, Wyoming.

Why this baby had brought up the past, he didn't know. Maybe simply because she *was* a baby. It was a good reason to stay away from her and the case. An even better reason was his adrenaline-rush attraction to Gwen Langworthy. Okay, so maybe his hammering had made her approach inaudible. But *nobody* had ever snuck up on him like that before without his gut alerting him. On top of that, he'd been so rattled he'd let her follow him to the house. He *always* covered his tail. He *never* let anyone get behind him.

Old habits died hard.

As a nurse exited the nursery, Garrett approached her. Her name tag read Dianne Spagnola, R.N. Her gaze ran over his black jeans and snap-button shirt.

"I'm sorry to bother you, but I'm working on the Baby Amy case with the sheriff's department." He and the sheriff weren't working on it together, but they *were* both working on it. "How's she doing?"

"I can't give out any information," the nurse said solemnly, "Not to anyone without written authorization."

Regulations and security were much tighter than they used to be. That was a good thing.

He motioned to the little girl. "She looks healthy, and she's not in isolation. From what I understand, she's waiting for a family. Gwen Langworthy told me that. You know, the woman who found her?"

The woman's shoulders seemed to relax a bit. "You know Gwen?"

He nodded.

"Amy's doing okay, eating better than she was. She needs a home."

"Can you tell me what happened to the clothes she was wearing when she was brought in?"

"Clothes?" the nurse asked, looking puzzled.

"Gwen told me she was wearing a playsuit with a sweater and hat." She had on one of those suits now, but it was pink, not yellow. "I wondered about the sweater and hat and the blanket she was wrapped in."

The nurse thought about it. "They might be in one of the storage closets."

If he took the case, he'd analyze them. If he took the case, he'd need to know the baby's blood type and whatever else her medical records could tell him. That would require a trip to the sheriff's office and legal maneuvering, *or* help behind the scenes.

If he took the case.

Handing Nurse Spagnola his business card, he asked, "Can you give me a call on my cell phone if you find the clothes? I'll be around town and can stop back."

The nurse checked his card and nodded.

Thanking her, he headed toward the elevator. Good old-fashioned footwork paid off in a town the size of Wild Horse Junction. He'd investigate a little more, then make up his mind.

Would *she* ever be a mom? Did she really believe a child needed *two* loving parents?

On Sunday morning after church, Gwen drove straight to the hospital to visit Baby Amy. It was simple and complicated at the same time. She considered herself a progressive woman. Yet she was discovering day by day she had very traditional values. On one hand, what if she never married? Why should she deny herself motherhood because a man didn't fit into her life…or she didn't fit into his? On the other hand, a picket fence and a partner for life was her deepest dream.

She'd stopped in to see Amy every day since the

baby had been deserted and, in spite of herself, Gwen felt a huge connection to the infant. When she held her and fed her and rocked her, she longed for her own baby as well as an ideal home for this one.

Today, instead of heading for the nursery, she stopped at the ob-gyn nurses' desk.

Dianne Spagnola looked up. "Gwen, do you know a Garrett Maxwell?"

"I know who he is," she answered. "Why?"

"Because he was here asking questions and gave me the impression he was working with the sheriff's department. After he left, I wondered if I should have told him anything."

Working with the sheriff's department. Her heart sped up with hope that he was going to take her case. "I asked him to help me find Amy's mother. He's on the level. How long ago was he here?"

"About ten minutes."

Maybe he was going to make up his mind before this evening. "Do you know which way he was headed?"

"He wanted me to see if I could find the clothes Amy was wearing when she was brought in. He gave me a card and told me to call his cell phone number. He said he'd be around town and he could stop back if I found them."

Around town. Wild Horse Junction wasn't that big. Maybe she could spot his SUV. It was huge and black and stark. She'd seen it in his driveway. There had been a decal on his side back window, a triangle with a small plane in its center. She'd wondered at the time if he belonged to some kind of club.

"I think I'm going to try to track him down." She gave Dianne a smile. "I'll be back to rock Amy in a little while."

"On our breaks, we give her as much attention as we can, but I think she likes you best."

After a quick goodbye, Gwen headed for the parking garage.

In her van, she decided to start with the main road in town, Wild Horse Way. As she drove south, she checked out the parking lots at the grocery store, restaurants and many shops that lined the street, catering to tourists— Flutes and Drums gallery, the Saddle Shop, the Turquoise Emporium. At the edge of town at a gas station combined with a convenience store, she spotted a black SUV. It looked like Garrett Maxwell's.

She pulled up beside it and saw the decal on the window. Pay dirt. After she pocketed her keys and picked up her purse, her heart raced faster and she told herself the increase was simply because she was anxious about him taking the case.

However, when she opened the door to the convenience store and saw him standing at the counter with the cashier, her attraction to him slammed into her full force. She'd always liked tall men, and he was definitely tall. He looked dangerous and sexy and she knew she should run in the other direction. But she needed his professional skill right now and she was going to get it if she could.

When he saw her, there was no simple "hello."

"This isn't a coincidence, is it?" he asked, brows raised.

She gave him a quick smile. "No. I went to the hospital."

"And?"

"And Dianne said you were asking questions and would be around town. Are you taking the case?"

"I'm still deciding." He turned his attention once again to the cashier. "So you don't remember a young couple?" he asked the teenager as if the boy had already said he didn't.

"Nope," the boy responded. "Who *are* you anyway? A cop?"

Not caring what Garrett Maxwell thought, Gwen interrupted, "Hi, Reuben. We met at the high school at the beginning of the month when I spoke to the senior class. You helped me with the screen in the auditorium."

The boy looked at her. "I remember. Ms. Langworthy, right?"

"Right. Reuben, do you remember a story in the paper about a baby that was found?"

"I don't read the paper much but my folks were talking about it."

"We're looking for that baby's mom."

"So you can arrest her?" he asked warily.

"No, we're not law enforcement. We want to find her so we can help her."

Although the teenager looked unsure for a few moments, he stared at Gwen and seemed to decide that she was sincere. Still he asked, "Help her, how?"

"We need to know why she left her baby." More times than Gwen could count she'd wondered about her own real mother. How young had she been? How rich or poor? Had there been no one to help her or had she simply not cared enough to keep a child? Had she shirked responsibility or simply been unable to accept it?

Shaking off those questions, she went on, "If she wants to give the baby up for adoption, that's fine. But we want to make sure she has the information she needs to make that decision. And if she really does want to be a mom, but needs help, we need to know that, too."

His gaze went to Garrett, then back to her. "Yeah, I guess you do. I don't know anything for sure."

"But you know something?" Gwen asked gently.

"Maybe. I was working Monday night. I only work Monday, Wednesday and Sunday. Anyway, this guy and his girl came in. The girl, she bought acetaminophen and those...those pads girls wear when they get their period. I remember her because she didn't look so good, really white, like she was going to pass out or something. When they left, the guy had his arm around her. You know, holding her up a little."

Garrett's gaze met Gwen's. Monday night was the night she'd found Amy, and this couple sounded like "the" couple.

"Can you describe them for me?" Garrett asked.

After hesitating a few moments, Reuben finally said, "She had long brown hair. He was a blonde."

"Did you notice what kind of car they were driving?" Garrett inquired.

The boy shrugged. "It chugged pretty much when the guy started it. I looked outside. It was a brown pickup truck—small, pretty battered up."

"Anything identifiable on it?" Garrett asked.

"Nah. I didn't see it up close."

"Which way did they go?"

"They headed north."

When Gwen exchanged a look with Garrett, he handed Reuben a business card. "If you remember anything else, give me a call, okay?"

The teenager nodded, and Garrett motioned for Gwen to go outside.

Next to a vending machine, she stopped. Garrett did, too, but he remained silent.

Facing him, her arm brushed his. As a buzz of attraction hummed between them, she asked, "That's our couple, don't you think? What do we do next?"

"What do you mean—what do *we* do next?" he asked warily. "You do whatever *you* do on Sundays and I'll continue what *I'm* doing."

Maybe he was a loner, but two heads were better than one. "Are you going to take the case?"

Though the nerve in his jaw worked, his tone was even. "I'm just doing some preliminary work to find out if there's a *reason* to take the case."

"You only search for someone when you know you'll be successful?" she challenged him.

His splayed fingers ran through his hair as if he were frustrated with her beyond measure. "No, of course not."

"Then, Mr. Maxwell, why is this such a hard decision to make?"

Although his penetrating stare might have made a lesser woman crumble, she didn't crumble, not even under the appraisal of a tough-guy former FBI agent.

Finally he replied, "It's a hard decision to make because I'm one person and I have a limited amount of time."

She certainly understood that. "Did you see Amy?"

His expression didn't change but something in his eyes did. "Yes, I saw her."

"We can't let that little girl go through life not knowing who her parents are."

"We?" he drawled again, his brows arched.

"Mr. Maxwell—" she began.

"It's Garrett."

"Garrett," she repeated, liking the sound of his name on her lips, liking the look of him, *not* liking the horribly exciting pull she felt toward him. "You wouldn't have started asking questions if you didn't want to help me with Amy."

"I wasn't getting very far until you came along," he acknowledged with a bit of chagrin.

"Reuben thought you were a cop. Kids his age don't rat on each other, not to someone in authority."

"I have a feeling you can get your way with the male species when you ratchet up the charm," Garrett commented.

How wrong he was about that! She hadn't had enough charm to keep Mark. Over and over she'd asked herself what she'd lacked...where she'd gone wrong...what need of his she hadn't satisfied.

"And if charm doesn't get you what you want, solid determination will," he went on, not looking happy about it.

"You've made this analysis when we've been in each other's company a total of what? Fifteen minutes?"

"Am I wrong?" he fired back.

That he'd pegged her so well in such a short amount of time was unnerving. "No, you're not wrong, but all my charm and all my determination won't find Amy's mother if I don't know what questions to ask or where to look."

Blowing out a breath, Garrett gazed in the direction of the Painted Peaks. The blue-shadowed, rust, gray and red mountains chased each other higher on the out- skirts of town. "Did you have lunch yet?" he asked.

That question was unexpected. "No, I haven't."

"Let's go to The Silver Dollar, get something to eat and talk about this."

The hope that he was really going to help her almost made her feel giddy. "All right. That sounds good to me."

Afraid he'd change his mind, she was starting for her car when he reached out and snagged her arm. There it was again—that snap and crackle of heat.

"Just because we look for Amy's mom doesn't mean we'll find her. More often than not, leads turn into dead ends," he warned her with the edge of experience in his statement.

"And sometimes, leads turn into other leads," she protested quietly.

With a shake of his head, his mouth turned up slightly at the corners. "Are you a Pollyanna?"

Because of the way she'd grown up, she was far from that. "No, but I make a conscious decision each morning to look at the brighter side of life and I think that pays off."

When he dropped his hand to his side, she felt its absence.

"I'll meet you at The Silver Dollar," he said gruffly, then stepped down off the curb and climbed into his SUV. After waiting for her to start up her van, he followed her.

She found herself smiling as she drove. Since when had lunch at The Silver Dollar seemed like a main event? Since Garrett Maxwell had extended the invitation.

Not knowing what in the hell he was going to do with Gwen Langworthy, Garrett noticed her terrifically long legs covered by her deep violet slacks, the sway of her breasts and hips under her sweater. He spotted an empty table and they headed for it.

The Silver Dollar was three-quarters full. It was a nice-sized restaurant decorated with ranch brands and lariats on the walls, alongside framed signed photographs of Roy Rogers and Gene Autry. But the western atmosphere barely registered as Garrett pulled out Gwen's chair for her.

Damn, she got to him in a way Cheryl never had. She was pushier than his ex-wife, franker, definitely more determined. In spite of himself, he wanted to know more about her and that was a big mistake. If he took this case, he'd just have to stay away from her.

If he took this case? He was already hooked and he knew it.

Stay away from Gwen Langworthy, he repeated to himself as if he had to translate the words from a foreign language. Standing behind her, looking down at her shiny auburn curls, all he wanted to do was sink his fingers into them. Well, that wasn't *all* he wanted to do.

Swiftly moving away from her perfume that smelled fruity and flowery all at the same time, he took the chair across from her and realized that his knees could too easily brush hers at the small table. It didn't take Yoda shaking a spiny finger at him to warn him not to engage in physical contact. May the Force be with him.

Before she opened her menu, her dark brown eyes met his. "How much do you charge?"

"I don't charge when I find children."

"As you pointed out, this isn't a child."

He shrugged. "Same difference this time."

"I can't let you—"

He dismissively brushed her words away. "You're not letting me do anything, and as I told you before, we might not find her."

"If this takes your time away from your other work, I need to reimburse you…for something."

"Let's just see where it goes. My workload is moderate right now." It would be until he heard the decision on the government contract he'd bid on.

She leaned forward a little. "The article I read said you do security consulting work. What exactly is that?"

"It varies."

When her eyes were still questioning, he knew she was going to come up with another inquiry. He remembered that determination he'd pegged in her. "I develop firewalls that are hacker-proof, along with suggesting physical systems for particular needs."

"You make Web sites secure? So that if I use my credit card number, nobody can filch it?"

"Something like that."

"Is that what you did for the FBI?"

Now she was treading into territory where he didn't want to go. "The skills I used in the FBI were varied." If his job had only been concerned with Internet security maybe Cheryl wouldn't have divorced him...maybe she wouldn't have lost their child.

"Classified?" she asked as if she knew what that was all about.

He laughed. "Let's just call it that and say the subject's off-limits."

But she didn't stop probing. "For personal or professional reasons?"

It was time he stopped her get-to-know-you session, although at some point he hoped to turn the tables on her. He didn't see a ring on her finger and wondered if she was involved with anyone.

"This conversation has nothing to do with Baby Amy, and that's who we came here to talk about."

"All right," she acquiesced begrudgingly. "What are we going to do next?"

Gazing into Gwen's beautiful dark brown eyes, he almost lost his train of thought. Focusing again, he answered her. "My guess is, the couple wasn't here more than a day. The fact that they bought the supplies they did at a convenience store rather than a grocery store or drugstore tells me they might have been passing through, maybe living out of the kid's truck. Maybe the girl even had the baby in the truck."

"But if she wasn't from here, why would she leave the baby with *me?* How did she know who I was?"

"You tell me." He had an idea, but he wanted to see if he was right.

After Gwen fingered her menu and chewed on her lower lip—whether she knew it or not, the habit was damn sexy—she explained, "When I go to a town to set up a program, like Jackson Hole or Cheyenne, some-times there's an article in the paper about what I'm doing. But I don't think anyone would see that and decide to leave a baby with me."

"That depends. I imagine it's clearly stated that you're an obstetrical nurse practitioner. That would qualify you to take care of a child. My guess is, if she's not from Wild Horse Junction, the mother met you at one of your programs. I want you to make a list of any young girls you talked to within the past year."

"You've got to be kidding!"

"No, I'm not."

"But I usually don't know last names."

"I don't care. Just try to get down names and if you can, picture faces with the names."

Suddenly Gwen's serious expression was overtaken by a brilliant smile as she spotted somebody coming through the door. It was a couple with a baby who looked to be six to eight months old.

The tall, sandy-haired man carrying the child and the pretty woman beside him came straight to Gwen. The two women hugged while the man looked on patiently. Then Gwen gave him a hug, too, baby and all. "It's so good to see you. Are you all unpacked?"

"Almost," Gwen's friend answered with a sideways glance at Garrett. "We have decorating to do, though. We're using lots of Dylan's photographs, of course, but I need some sconces and hangings."

"She *really* needs them," the sandy-haired man joked, trying to suppress a smile.

His wife playfully swatted his arm.

Before the conversation developed further, Gwen gestured to Garrett, who had stood.

"This is Garrett Maxwell. He's helping me find Baby Amy's mother. Garrett, this is Shaye and Dylan Malloy and their son Timmy. Shaye is the social worker I called."

Now the puzzle pieces fit. Garrett had seen the article in the *Wild Horse Wrangler* about Dylan Malloy's show at the Flutes and Drums Gallery and how successful it had been. The man was a top-notch wildlife photographer. Garrett also remembered the write-up on the accident that had taken the lives of Dylan's sister and brother-in-law in February. Timmy had been born right before his mother had died.

Garrett shook hands with the husband and wife. Timmy was a cute little guy with blond hair and green eyes, but he was already getting itchy, squirming in Dylan's arms.

"Okay, big fella," Dylan said. "We'll pick up dinner and go."

"We called after church," Shaye explained to Gwen. "We're taking a meal out to Kylie."

"I spoke to her last night," Gwen said. "I'm worried about her. Ever since Alex's funeral, she's been working twice as hard as she should while she's pregnant. Now at over five months, she should be slowing down."

"I know." Shaye shook her head. "That bull-riding accident didn't just end Alex's life, it left Kylie with a burden that's too big to handle on her own."

"That's why we're going out to Saddle Ridge," Dylan interjected. "She has a fence down and Dix hasn't had time to get to it. I'm no expert, but I can rig up something."

After realizing they were keeping Garrett out of the conversation, Gwen turned to him. "We have a friend who was widowed in July. She's taken on running the ranch with her foreman and it's a lot to handle, especially with her being pregnant."

The cashier near the door waved to Dylan and Shaye and motioned to the takeout containers on the counter.

As Timmy began to fuss louder, Dylan lifted him high and wiggled him a bit. "We're going. We're going."

Shaye gave Gwen's hand a squeeze. "I'll call you later."

After goodbyes all around, the Malloys went to the counter to pay for their dinner. Dylan's arm curved around his wife's waist as they waited for the cashier to ring up their food.

"They've only been married since July," Gwen told Garrett as she sat down once more. "They're still newlyweds."

"I imagine it's hard to be newlyweds with a baby." Garrett kept his tone even. When he thought about the child he'd lost before it even had a chance, his insides went cold.

"Timmy brought Shaye and Dylan together," Gwen explained. "So they cherish every day with him."

"Timmy was Dylan's sister's child?"

"Right. Are you from around here? Did you know Julia, Dylan's sister?"

"I was born here, but left when I was a teenager. Since I came back, I don't socialize much. I didn't know his sister."

"How long ago did you return?"

He wondered if he was attracted to Gwen *because*

she irritated him or in spite of the fact. "Do you always ask so many questions?"

Instead of being offended, she smiled sweetly. "How else am I going to learn what I want to know if I don't ask questions?"

Shaking his head, he had to chuckle. "I returned five years ago." Now he turned the beacon of questioning on *her* life. "How long have you and Shaye Malloy been friends?"

"Shaye and Kylie and I were pals in grade school. When Kylie skipped a grade, we kind of took her under our wings."

"Her husband died recently?"

"Shortly after Shaye and Dylan's wedding. We want to help her but she's so independent. She insists on doing everything herself. As her pregnancy gets further along, I don't know what she's going to do."

"I'm not sure I understand. Why can't she hire extra help?"

"Have you heard of Saddle Ridge Ranch?"

"Nothing lately. Jack Warner owned the place when I was younger. He raised cutting horses, didn't he?"

"Yes, but his son Alex—" Gwen abruptly stopped. "I shouldn't say anything else."

So Gwen wasn't a gossip and she was loyal to her friends. Most of the women he'd known had been very competitive and a little thing like friendship wouldn't have made a difference or gotten in the way of catching a man or achieving a higher level in a career.

The waitress came over to them and they quickly glanced at the menus and ordered. As they ate the special of the day—roast beef, mashed potatoes and a vegetable medley—Garrett noticed Gwen finished almost all of it.

"Do you work out?"

Laying down her fork, she wiped her mouth with her napkin. "I work out at the Wagon Wheel Fitness Center. Why?"

He couldn't help but grin. "Because it's been a long time since I saw a woman down mashed potatoes."

Spots of color came to her milky white cheeks that were dotted with a few freckles. "That's an advantage to working out, I guess. I eat pretty much what I want."

As his gaze passed over her pale lilac sweater and the way the material clung to her breasts, his jeans got tight and not from the food he was eating.

Retreating to safer territory, he remarked, "Now that Malloy's married, I wonder what will happen to his career." Garrett knew all about careers ruining marriages—first his dad's, then his own. The thing was he'd become an FBI agent for a good reason and the idea of giving up his mission had been unthinkable. If his friend hadn't been kidnapped when they were both nine, if he hadn't felt a moral calling to right the world's wrongs, maybe he could have given up his vocation and put all of his passion into his marriage. Maybe.

"He's changing how he works," Gwen admitted. "He's contracted for a book about the wild mustangs and another one on whales in Alaska. He's determined not to let his work get in the way of his marriage."

"Work can do that," Garrett muttered softly.

"Yours got in the way of a relationship?"

"Mine ended my marriage." It was the first he'd ever said it out loud to another living person, and why he'd said it here, now, to Gwen Langworthy, he didn't know. He didn't like not knowing.

Picking up the bill the waitress had left on the table, he glanced at it, pulled out his wallet, left a tip, stood and said, "I'll take care of this. I want to ask the cashier a few questions."

The restaurant had emptied out and the cashier sat on the stool by the register, reading a romance novel. Romance might come alive in books, but that was the only place anybody would find it, Garrett decided as he made his way to her.

By the time the cashier closed the book and stood, Gwen was by his side, the fruity-flowery scent of her annoying him, her energy invigorating him, her beauty capturing him. He fought against the capture.

He was aware of Gwen watching him while he paid the bill. She was such a distraction, he wanted to put her outside while he completed his questioning. But he knew she wouldn't stand for that.

A few minutes later, to his surprise and Gwen's, the cashier described the couple in more detail than the teenager at the convenience store, then pointed them toward the waitress who had been on duty that night.

Mandy Jacobs remembered the couple. But foremost on her mind was batting her lashes at Garrett and flirting with him for all she was worth. "The girl had soup and the cute guy had a burger. They didn't leave a tip, that's why I remember them so well. That's about all I know.

I'll ask around, Mr. Maxwell. I'll be *sure* to contact you if any of the other girls saw anything or remember more than I do."

"That would be great," he told her, handing her his card. "We appreciate all the help we can get."

Fluttering her lashes at him a few more times, she encouraged him, "You be sure to sit at *my* table next time you come in."

"I'll be sure to do that," Garrett returned with a smile.

Gwen hadn't said a word during the interchange and as they stepped outside, she muttered, "Talk about charm."

"She probably does that with every man she waits on. Better tips."

"You didn't do anything to discourage her."

Unreasonably, Garrett felt a bit of male satisfaction at Gwen's comment. "She could have had information I needed, and she still could find out something. You just never know."

Stopping, he took Gwen's arm. "Why would it bother you if she was flirting with me?"

"It didn't bother me," Gwen protested quickly. "But she's an impressionable young girl and if you give her hope…"

"The Silver Dollar doesn't hire anybody under eighteen so she's not so young—not the way you mean, anyway. And…I never encourage anything more than answers to my questions."

When Gwen studied him for a very long time, he asked, "Are you involved with anyone?"

"No."

"Did you have a marriage that went south, too?"

After a brief hesitation, she answered, "No, I didn't get that far. My fiancé stood me up at the altar."

"On your wedding day?" Garrett was truly astonished by that piece of background.

"On my wedding day. And I don't intend to ever let that happen again. I'll never again depend on a man to make me happy or trust a man the way I trusted Mark." Moving away from him, maybe embarrassed because she'd said too much, she pointed to the decal on his SUV. "What's that for?"

"I belong to a network of pilots who help with search and rescue. That's our logo."

"You're a pilot?"

He nodded.

"Do you have your own plane?"

"I inherited my dad's."

"You lost him?" she asked so sympathetically he was reminded she'd known loss, too, albeit in a different way.

"Yes. Seven years ago. In some ways it seems like yesterday and in others it seems like forever." When his parents divorced, he'd gone to live with his father. College had only been two years away and the judge had acceded to Garrett's wishes to move to L.A. with his father rather than to Wisconsin with his mother. Losing his dad to cancer had been a blow he hadn't expected.

"Do you still have your mom?"

"I sure do. She lives in Wisconsin now, and if I don't faithfully call once a week, she worries."

His gaze on Gwen, he watched as a wave of sadness passed over her face. Was it the reference to motherhood? But before he could probe a bit, she said, "You're a complicated man."

"No more complicated than *you* are." Knowing that their conversation would soon lead to more personal territory that was better left unexplored, he asked, "Where are you going now?"

"Back to the hospital. I want to hold Amy for a bit."

Immediately, he could envision Gwen holding that precious child and the turmoil inside him was too stormy to analyze. "I'll follow you there. A nurse was going to see if she could find the clothes Amy was wearing the night she was brought in."

"I wonder why the sheriff didn't take them. He looked at them, but didn't take them."

"I don't know what that was all about, but then Sheriff Thompson is near retirement age," Garrett noted. "I'm not sure how much effort he puts into his work. We've butted heads a couple of times so I stay clear of him if I can. But I might have to pay him a visit."

They stood at Garrett's SUV by the side of the building. Nobody came and went. Once in a while a few cars traveled up and down the street as the wind whipped Gwen's curls across her cheek. Without forethought Garrett reached out to stroke them away.

He should have known better than to touch her.

Her eyes became luminescent and softly deep. The urge to kiss her was so strong, he could taste it. He could feel it in every part of his body, especially the ones that mattered. He stepped even closer…bent his head…

The sun, which had been hiding behind a cloud, suddenly shone brightly and illuminated Gwen, sending firelight through her hair, giving him clarity about what he should and shouldn't do.

As if the sun had cleared up things for Gwen, too, she took a step back and gave him a weak smile. "Amy's waiting for me. Maybe I'll see you at the hospital."

While she was opening the door to her van and he was opening the door to his SUV, he realized it would be better if he *didn't* see Gwen at the hospital.

It would be better if he found Amy's mother on his own.

Chapter Three

Gwen was taking clothes from her washer and pushing them into her dryer when her doorbell rang. She was expecting Garrett.

She had intended to ignore him yesterday at the hospital but he'd poked his head into the nursery and told her the nurses couldn't find Amy's clothes. They were going to keep looking and notify either him or Gwen if they found anything. When Gwen had stopped to see Amy over her lunch hour today, the desk nurse had handed her a bag. Someone had found the clothes in a supply cupboard. Immediately Gwen had called Garrett.

Her heart beating harder, she pushed he dryer door closed with a bang and hurried to the door.

What had almost happened between her and Garrett

*yesterday? Had it been an almost kiss? If so, she had
pulled away from it, hadn't she?*

Gwen gave herself a mental shake and told herself
to slow down. She didn't get infatuated with men, she
reminded herself. She was picky, and a rugged face
with a good body might turn her head, but it didn't stay
turned. She wanted substance.

You thought you had substance with Mark, a little
voice reminded her.

She'd been so wrong about that. She'd been so wrong
about a lot of things. She had taken a close look at
herself and her choices since Mark left and she hadn't
liked some of the things she'd seen. But she was
working on fixing them, working on breaking away
from a childhood she had no control over, working on
an adult, stable relationship with her dad.

As she opened the door to Garrett, common sense
flew out the proverbial window. He was a hottie, plain
and simple. She was attracted to him, plain and simple.
She would watch every step she made, plain and
simple. Tonight he wore gray dress slacks with a west-
ern-cut white shirt and a bolo tie. Her surprise must
have shown.

"I clean up now and then," he said with a dark sardonic
smile that fired up the quick thrill of excitement running
through her at seeing him. "I had a meeting in Cody."

"Sorry, I didn't mean to stare," she admitted, her
cheeks hot. "Come on in," she said quickly to cover her
embarrassment.

When she'd gotten home from work, she'd made a
chocolate bundt cake. It was sitting in a cake holder on

her table with powdered sugar sprinkled across the top. She hadn't baked for herself.

"Would you like some coffee? I have chocolate cake, too, if you're interested."

Stopping short of her kitchen, he seemed to weigh whether he wanted to accept her offer or not. "I grabbed supper at a fast-food restaurant before I left Cody. But chocolate cake is hard to turn down."

"Is that a yes? The coffee's fresh, I made it with supper. It's Kona," she added, nonchalantly, knowing that would be an additional enticement for a coffee lover.

"Where did you get Kona here?"

"I have my sources." As she gathered dishes from the cupboard and silverware from the drawer, she motioned to her mug tree. "Go ahead and pour yourself a cup. I'll cut the cake."

When she removed the glass cover, he looked at the cake and then glanced at her. "Did you bake that for tonight?"

She could say she always had baked goods around to nibble on, but that would be a lie. "Yes. Most men like chocolate."

At her elbow, he capped her shoulder. "Gwen—"

"Look, it was no trouble. If you won't let me pay you, I have to reimburse you somehow. A snack just seemed hospitable."

Before, when she'd been close to Garrett, she'd caught the scent of man and the outdoors. Now she noticed his cologne. It was lime and musky and compelling…just as he was. His gray eyes seemed heated with an inner fire as he studied her. She wondered if they were both thinking about lips touching, tongues entwining, sex in the dark of night. His beard line was shadowed now at the end of the day. To her dismay she realized how much she'd like to touch it...how much she'd like to feel it on her skin.

Although the fire in his eyes wasn't banked, his tone was neutral as he shifted slightly away from her and asked, "Do you have Amy's clothes?"

The mention of the infant made her take a resigned breath and remember exactly why he was here. This wasn't a tea party...or a coffee party.

Motioning to the cake, she suggested, "Go ahead and cut yourself a slice while I get them."

When she would have stepped away, she heard him mutter, "Oh, hell."

The next moment, his hand was on her shoulder, he was bending his head, and his lips came down hard on hers.

Garrett's lips were as hot as the sizzle of attraction between them. Gwen's hand rested against his chest, and she ran her fingers up the placket of his shirt to the taut skin of his neck. His hair was shaggy over his collar, thick and coarse. When his tongue slid into her mouth, the erotic sensation of it almost made her gasp. The hunger and desire in his kiss fired a like hunger and desire in her. Her last coherent thought was a simple one—*this is pure chemistry.*

When his tongue danced with hers, time was suspended and she practically melted at his feet. The passion blooming inside of her was overwhelming, and she wondered why it had lain dormant all her life until this moment.

However, as quickly as Garrett had decided to kiss her, he decided to stop kissing her.

Thank goodness his hands were on her shoulders to steady her or she might have collapsed. With a monumental effort, she took a step away from him, testing the steadiness of her knees.

"Wow!" She didn't know exactly what else to say and that seemed to say it all.

On his part, Garrett didn't seem to be as affected as she was. In fact...

"I shouldn't have done that."

He looked so composed she wanted to beat on his chest and ask him, *Wasn't that just the best kiss you ever had?* She'd never experienced anything like it with Mark...or anyone else. However, just because Garrett had turned her kitchen upside down for her didn't mean she'd done the same to him.

"Why not?" she blurted out. "Are you involved with someone?" That wouldn't be a first. Men were notorious for wanting to sample greener grass...or nostalgic grass. Not a month after she and Mark had broken up, she'd learned he was dating his former girlfriend. Had they been in touch while he and Gwen were engaged? When they had talked after his defection, Mark had denied that anyone else had been involved. But he had gotten married six months later, so Gwen suspected otherwise.

"No, I'm not involved," Garrett snapped. "And I don't intend to *be* involved. That's the point."

His blunt assessment put her in her place. "I see," she murmured. "That's good. Because I don't want to be involved, either. Your cologne must have fogged my brain." Then before he could comment on that bit of nonsense, she turned away and headed for the living room. "I'll get the clothes."

Her hands trembled slightly as she went to the rolltop desk and lifted the lid. Garrett followed her, obviously forgetting about cake and coffee. To her dismay, her shoulder grazed his as she turned around. He was too big, too close, and too intense. Obviously too emotionally unavailable.

When she couldn't find anything else to add to the mental list of reasons why she shouldn't get involved with him, she thrust the grocery bag toward him. "Here."

Eyeing her as if he wanted to ask her about something, yet didn't want to deal with her answers after the asking, he took the white grocery bag. Spilling the contents, he first examined the blanket including the tag sewn into the hem. After he laid that across the top of the desk chair, he looked over the terry playsuit. Setting that aside, he studied the tiny knitted sweater and cap.

As he fingered them, he asked, "Do you know anything about yarn?"

She blinked. "Yarn?"

"This doesn't look and feel like the usual acrylic."

Taking the sweater fabric between her fingers herself, she noticed that it indeed didn't. The yarn was fine, coated by a soft cloudy fuzziness.

"I want to take these along," he said, stuffing everything back in the bag, plucking the sweater from her hands.

Their fingertips brushed.

When she looked up into Garrett's eyes, they were turbulent and for the most part, unreadable.

Her doorbell rang and she jumped. That was so not like her. Composure was her middle name. This man shook her up and flustered her and she didn't like that at all.

"Are you expecting anyone?" he asked.

"No. But it could be Kylie or Shaye. We drop in on each other." Then glad to put some space between them, she went to her door and opened it.

Her father stood there.

"Hi, Dad. This is a surprise." She stepped back so he could come inside.

When he did, she studied him for the telltale signs he'd fallen off the wagon. It was a habit with her.

To her relief he was dressed neatly in jeans and a denim jacket. His eyes were clear. With his burnished red hair streaked with gray and his blue eyes, he'd once been a charmer and a very handsome man. That was before alcohol, regret and guilt had added lines to his face that had aged him at least ten years. He was fifty-eight now and selling insurance. Although he'd once been an accountant, after Gwen had left and he sobered up, he decided he liked being out and around people.

Seeing Garrett, her dad flushed slightly. "I didn't mean to interrupt anything. If you want me to go—"

Bag in hand, Garrett came over to where they were standing. "No need for that. I was just leaving."

The two men could have passed like the proverbial ships in the night, but Gwen felt the need to introduce them to each other. "Garrett Maxwell, this is my father, Russ Langworthy. Dad, Garrett is helping me find Amy's mother."

Garrett's brow arched as if she should have put that

a different way, but she didn't care. They were working together on this whether he liked it or not.

"I've heard about you," Russ said, extending his hand.

Garrett shook it with a smile. "Do I want to know what you've heard?"

Her father laughed. "Mostly rumors. That you live in the hills, stick to yourself, and you used to be FBI. This is Wild Horse Junction, boy. A kernel of truth gets embellished and goes a long way."

"What you heard is true."

"Besides the gossip, I remember your parents. Your dad was a commercial pilot. How are they? I heard after they divorced, your mom moved to Wisconsin and you and your dad to California."

"Dad passed away some years back. Mom's still in Wisconsin."

"Dad, Garrett has to be going," Gwen intervened. She suspected Garrett wasn't the type of man to talk about his personal life easily.

"It's okay," Garrett assured her, but his body was a little more rigid than it had been a few minutes before.

"I'm sorry to hear about your dad." After an awkward pause, Russ said, "Divorce is tough on kids. It was tough on Gwen, especially her mother's move to Indiana," he explained. "How old were you when your parents separated? Around fifteen?"

"Dad," Gwen protested fiercely before Garrett could answer.

That wasn't a subject Gwen wanted to discuss with either Garrett or her father. Long ago she'd dealt with the abandonment by her biological parents, but her adopted mother's defection had been much harder. Not only had Myra Langworthy divorced her dad, but she'd divorced Gwen, too. All she'd cared about was the man she'd fallen in love with and the new family she'd begun with him in Indiana. Gwen had felt like an outsider on her few visits there, and had lived in quiet misery with her dad, wondering why her adoptive mother hadn't loved her enough to want her in her life in a meaningful way.

Rerouting her father's frame of mind, Gwen said to him, "I have cake and coffee if you're interested."

"I'm always interested in cake and coffee." Letting the subject stray from Garrett, he lifted a pamphlet in his hand. "I brought a brochure about a cruise I'm thinking of taking. I'd like your opinion on it." To Garrett he said, "It was good to meet you." With a glance at the kitchen, he told her, "I'll go start on that cake," and then he left them alone while he ambled into the other room.

"I'm sorry about the questions," Gwen said as soon as her dad was out of earshot.

"Your father was just making conversation."

"Maybe." She never knew exactly what her dad was thinking, let alone what he'd do next.

After studying her for a few moments, Garrett asked, "How old were *you* when your parents divorced?"

Did she want to talk about this with Garrett? She only hesitated a few moments. "I was six—too young to understand, yet old enough to know my life was changed irrevocably…just like Dad's."

Shaking off the melancholy she often felt when examining memories of those years after the divorce, she gestured to the bag in Garrett's hand. "Let me know what you find out about that, okay?"

"How do you know I'm going to find out anything?"

"Because you already have an idea about the yarn."

"Were you a private investigator in your past life?" he asked sarcastically.

"Nope, but I watch *CSI*."

When he laughed, she liked the sound of it. She liked way too much about him.

"I'll let you know what happens."

Their gazes locked for a few interminable moments and she vividly remembered everything about their kiss, about him holding her, about him backing away. The chemistry between them was so hot, it had burned away memories of Mark's defection. Even so, in another few moments, *she* would have ended the kiss and backed away. At least that's what she told herself.

Garrett opened the door and without a goodbye, he stepped into the cloudless night. Deep down Gwen knew he was a much different kind of man than her ex-fiancé. Garrett was intense…focused…and passionate. She closed the door behind him.

Maybe cake and coffee with her dad would help her find her equilibrium. Maybe it would help alleviate the worry that was always with her that he would fall off the wagon again.

"We shouldn't have come," Gwen said. "You're tired."

On Thursday evening, Gwen and Shaye sat in Kylie's living room while she brought them glasses of iced tea. She'd insisted on getting it herself. Almost six months pregnant now, she was wearing a maternity top with her jeans. She looked tired and Gwen couldn't imagine her friend trying to keep up with the chores on the ranch, work a job in town and take care of herself, too.

Sitting on a teal-and-wine striped chair with huge rolled arms that seemed to swallow her, Kylie protested, "I'm fine."

"You've got to take care of yourself," Shaye suggested gently, "*and* the baby."

"I'm doing that. I try to be finished in the barn by nine, so I'm getting a good night's sleep." Kylie had pulled her long, straight blond hair back into a ponytail and her blue eyes under her bangs seemed to hold constant worry now.

"I hope you're not doing any heavy lifting," Gwen scolded, noticing that the plasma screen TV Alex had bought to study his rodeo technique was gone.

"Dix won't let me. You know that."

Dix Pepperdale had been foreman of Saddle Ridge Ranch since long before Jack Warner, Kylie's father-in-law, had died. He looked on Kylie as a daughter and was protective of her.

"How's the new mustang?" Gwen asked.

"Great." Suddenly Kylie brightened. "Feather isn't afraid of me now, at least not as afraid as she was. I hope this week I can get her to eat out of my hand."

Kylie had adopted a wild mustang from those that ran free in the Big Horn Mountains. When the Bureau of Land Management thinned the herd, they sold them at auction.

"She's really helping me cope...with Alex being gone," Kylie added. "It's so odd. I *do* miss him. Even though I was thinking about leaving him, before we were married we were friends for so many years."

When Gwen thought about Alex, she pictured a charming cowboy who'd never grown up. His parents had pampered him. He'd pampered himself. He hadn't been ready for marriage, not a real marriage where commitment was all-important. Kylie had found that out too late.

"Have you heard from Brock?" Shaye asked.

Kylie hesitated a few moments. "He called a few days after the funeral."

It was unusual that Kylie hadn't told them that before now.

"I had his address in Texas and I called there, leaving a message for him to phone me," Kylie went on. "He didn't get it until after the funeral. He was in some jungle looking for oil. It wasn't until he got back to base camp that he found my message."

"Did you tell him you were pregnant?" Gwen asked. Kylie had taken the job as horse trainer at Saddle Ridge when she was seventeen. Since she lived on-site she had run into Alex's older half brother Brock whenever he had come home from college. Gwen knew that when Kylie was younger, she'd thought Brock Warner had walked on water.

After a few moments of hesitation, Kylie answered, "Yes, I told him I'm pregnant, and I learned something Alex hadn't told me."

Suspecting there were lots of things Alex hadn't told his wife, Gwen asked, "What?"

"Brock's been divorced for over a year."

The silence in the room was filled with Kylie's

sadness. Brock had an Apache heritage and had felt like a second-class citizen at the ranch, especially since Jack Warner had always treated Alex like the golden son. Brock had made his own way as a geologist in Texas.

"I told Brock everything here was fine. I couldn't tell him the truth. I need time. I have to get the ranch built up again. It's my child's future."

"What are you going to do if Brock comes back here and wants you to sell it?" Always the realist, Gwen knew Jack Warner's will had put Kylie in a pickle. He'd left the ranch to Alex as long as Alex lived there and ran it. If he ever sold it, half the proceeds went to Brock. The same would now apply to Kylie.

"I really can't think about that now. I sold the TV," she said, her hand fluttering toward the place where the screen had once hung. "I'm using that for expenses. I listed the mechanical bull on eBay and I'm hoping I'll get a good price on it. If I can sell that, it will help me pay the back taxes. The cattle won't bring in enough this year."

"Maybe I can take my vacation after the baby's born and come out here and help you," Gwen offered.

Kylie's eyes misted with tears and she brushed them away. "Thank you, but we'll wait and see. If I get a few more horses to board that could make up for the training money I'm losing while I'm pregnant. I can't risk a fall with this baby to think about."

"You still have a stockpile of quilts. You could sell more of those."

"I sold a few to buy Feather and to use for vet bills. I'm saving the others for emergencies."

One of Kylie's quilt designs hung on the wall along

with photo collages of the Warner family and a...dream catcher. Gwen hadn't seen that before.

Taking out a tissue and blowing her nose, Kylie repocketed it in her jeans. "So how's your FBI agent working out?" she asked, obviously tired of being the center of attention.

"That's a good question," Gwen joked. "I haven't heard from him since Monday and I don't know if he's made more progress. I left a message yesterday but he hasn't returned my call."

"And you're not going to stand for that," Shaye said with a smile.

Gwen laughed. "Actually, no, I'm not. I think I'm going to drive out there tonight after I drop you off."

"We know you don't let grass grow under your feet," Kylie teased.

No, she didn't. Tonight she'd be seeing Garrett Maxwell whether he was ready to see *her* again or not.

Gwen was hopeful when she spied a small light burning in Garrett's loft. It had to be the loft from the way the first floor looked simply fuzzy with light. She supposed he could leave it on when he was away. Did men care about walking into a dark house? Maybe if she could understand questions like that, she could understand men.

She obviously hadn't understood Mark or she would have seen the signs that he was going to cut and run. The problem was—she'd had a lot of people cut and run from her, without any signs.

Casting those thoughts aside, she stepped onto the

porch and rang the bell. A few moments later she rang it again.

Suddenly there Garrett was—rumpled, hair tousled, shirt open down the front. He looked as if he'd been…sleeping? The stubble of his beard told her he hadn't even shaved today.

At a loss for words, she just stood there and stared.

"I fell asleep on the couch."

Although he might have been asleep when she rang the bell, he was fully alert now.

"I…uh…you didn't return my calls."

He ran his hand over his face. "I was going to. I got back from a search and rescue around six. I intended to rest on the sofa for a couple minutes, but…" He checked his watch with a luminescent dial. "I guess it's more like hours than minutes. Come on in."

She'd been right about the light in the loft. The living room was hazy with shadows.

When he strode to a side table, Gwen noticed his feet were bare. He switched on the wrought-iron based lamp. A yellow glow splashed over the rust-colored leather sofa where a wool throw was twisted into a ball.

Opening her suede jacket, but leaving it on, she sat in the nubby-textured recliner. "Where were you searching?"

"Near Yellowstone. A boy camping with his family. We found him late this afternoon."

"He's all right?"

"Shaken up, thirsty and hungry, but he was okay. He'd been missing twenty-four hours and his parents were crazy with worry." Garrett's fingers went to his jawline. "That's why I look like I just stepped out of the wilderness."

He looked exactly like that and so sexy her stomach was jumping all over the place. Deciding honesty was the best policy, especially with Garrett, she admitted, "I'm sorry I bothered you. But when you didn't answer my calls, I thought you were avoiding me."

"I was," he answered tersely. "I didn't have any news about Amy's mother, and after that kiss, I knew things would be strained between us."

She wasn't sure what she was feeling was "strain." It was more like a humming that affected her whole body. The question was—did Garrett feel the humming, too? But even if he did, he wasn't the type of man she wanted to get involved with. She wanted an open book. She wanted someone who could share and communicate and be affectionate and not hide his innermost thoughts. She suspected this man had a lot of practice hiding feelings, thoughts, and maybe even who he was.

"Whether there's a strain between us or not, I need to know if you made any progress," she assured him.

He was still standing and he seemed to debate with himself. "Why don't you make yourself at home in my kitchen. There's hot chocolate in one of the canisters beside the mugs. I'll get a quick shower, then we can talk. Unless you don't have time."

"I have time," she said softly, eager to hear what Garrett had to say, eager to get to know just a little bit more about him...just a *little* bit more.

Ten minutes later Garrett was back downstairs, picking up the mug of hot chocolate she'd prepared for him. "Thanks," he said, a half smile curving his lips. With his damp, wavy hair and in his tan knit shirt and jeans, she wanted to dive into his arms. She had to get a grip.

Taking their mugs into the living room, he tossed aside the throw and sank down beside her on the sofa. The humming was definitely still there.

After he set his mug on the coffee table, he leaned back. "I did find out some information. Not enough to move on, though, yet. I sent the yarn to a fiber special-ist to be analyzed and identified. I've made contacts who owe me," he explained. "The good news is—only one store in Wyoming ordered it…in Laramie. The bad news is—the owner of that store is overhauling her computer system and it won't be up and running again until next week. She's going to e-mail me when she finds the names of the purchasers."

In spite of herself, Gwen had been hoping for more. "Meantime, Amy might be placed with a family. Shaye is having an interview tomorrow with a couple."

Gwen had taken off her jacket in the kitchen and left it over a chair. Now her shoulder was almost brushing Gar-rett's. Neither of them moved away from the close contact.

When he shifted toward her, his body tensed. "This isn't science, Gwen. Sometimes I have to count on sheer luck. The best situation for that child might be to place her with a couple."

"I know that. It's just—"

"You identify with this baby," he suggested gently. "Your birth parents abandoned you, and from what your father said, I gathered your adopted mother did, too."

"She didn't abandon me, exactly. She left me with my father."

"She didn't take you along, and that's what a mother should do. When my parents divorced, I was old enough to make a choice. I decided to go to California with my dad. But at six, I imagine you wanted to be with your mother."

"What Dad and I wanted didn't matter. All that mattered to her was the new man she fell in love with."

"Your dad said she moved to Indiana." Again his voice was quiet, almost kind.

"Peter, her new husband, had family there. They decided a fresh start was best for everybody. But it wasn't. The night she left, Dad started drinking and didn't stop until three years ago."

"Whatever happened three years ago must have been earth shattering to him if he stopped." Garrett's interested statement urged her to go on.

"I'd never realized it, but all those years I took care of him, I was enabling him. Shaye and Kylie encouraged me to get counseling, so I finally went to a few Al-Anon meetings. I learned I had to change as much as he did. So, I did my own intervention of sorts. I told Dad I was moving out and buying a house and he was going to have to take care of his own bills. That meant he had to work regularly. He'd been an accountant up until then. He just took on work when he felt like it, or when he needed the money. I don't think he thought I was serious until I put a contract on a house, packed my things and then moved out. I had a neighbor check on him and for about a week, he drank even more. Then he checked himself into the rehab program at the hospital and started going to

AA meetings. All those years he drank, he'd stop now and then for a few weeks at a time, but then he'd pick up the bottle again. So now, I hold my breath and hope for the best. But I guess I'm always preparing myself for the worst."

"You did the right thing—making him responsible for his own life."

There was admiration in Garrett's voice. Kylie and Shaye had supported her through it all, but in the dead of night when she worried about her father, she felt alone. "I was so scared when I told him I was moving out. Afterward, I think my dad actually respected me more. The problem is with all those years of me taking up the slack between us, I think he knows I don't trust him to stay sober. We have surface conversation and walk on eggshells a lot of the time."

"Do you hear from your adoptive mother?"

"I get a Christmas card once a year," she said lightly as if it didn't hurt that her own mother didn't send letters or birthday cards. Except it wasn't her *own* mother. It was her adoptive mother.

"If I ever become a mom," Gwen murmured fiercely, "my child will know she's loved every minute of the day, every day of the year, for as long as she and I live. Even longer if I have anything to say about it."

When she looked into Garrett's eyes, she saw compassion there and it made her want to cry. She didn't cry. She hadn't cried much since she was six and her mother had left.

"I don't know why I told you all of this. I didn't mean to bend your ear."

"I have one to spare," he replied with a straight face and then smiled.

"You're a good listener. I guess you have to be to catch criminals."

He didn't comment.

"Right. That subject's off-limits. I guess I found out what I came here to find out." She knew she should stand, put on her jacket and leave. But she liked feeling Garrett's body heat. She liked the after-shower scent of soap and man. She liked the way he listened.

"You *will* call me when you get that e-mail?" she asked.

"I'll call you." He was silent for a while and the shadows in the room seemed to grow more intimate. All she could hear was the hum of the refrigerator, the creak of the house losing its heat from the day.

Suddenly he said, "There's a barn dance Saturday night on the Wilkins ranch. We're raising money to build an addition for the elementary school."

"You're involved in that?" He had the reputation for being a lone wolf, but there were causes he seemed to care passionately about.

"I'm giving a donation and that got me two tickets. If you have something better to do, that's fine."

He was making it sound as if it didn't matter if she said yes or not. "I'd like to go, but I don't remember how to square dance. I guess you do?"

"All you have to do is learn a few moves and you'll be fine. Are you good at following directions?"

"That depends," she drawled.

He chuckled, "On whether or not you *want* to follow the directions. That's all square dancing is—

following calls. They can come fast but pretty soon you'll catch on."

"Is this a date?" she asked lightly.

With a frown, he answered, "I'd rather not categorize it, but I'll pick you up and take you home." Then he put one knuckle under her chin and lifted it so she looked at him.

Was he going to kiss her again?

As his gaze roved over her face, she anticipated the feel of his lips, the stroke of his tongue, his calloused skin against hers. But he didn't kiss her. He dropped his hand and moved away.

Gwen told herself Saturday night might not be a date, but if she wasn't careful, it could be a disaster.

Chapter Four

Garrett had never intended to attend the barn dance. He'd certainly never intended to bring a date!

Yet here he was, spruced up in a brand new pair of black jeans, gray snap-button shirt and bolo tie, acting as if taking a woman to a dance was a common occurrence. Parked in a mown field with rows of other cars, he climbed out of his SUV and went around to Gwen's side. The sky was awash with orange and purple as the sun bobbed over the Painted Peaks.

Gwen had already opened her door when he got there, and he held out his hand to help her step down. She was wearing a denim dress with a hem trimmed in yellow-and-red flowers. She'd thrown a red shawl around her shoulders. He'd always heard redheads shouldn't wear red, but then she wasn't exactly a redhead. Her hair was a coppery color that was too rich to come out of a bottle.

Although Gwen settled her hand in his, she didn't step down right away. "Are you sure you want to do this? You didn't say a word on the drive over here. Maybe you regret asking me to come along?"

One thing he knew about Gwen Langworthy, she said what was on her mind. Maybe she could read minds, too.

"I invited you to come tonight. Why wouldn't I want to be here?"

"I don't know. Why *wouldn't* you?" she returned.

"Maybe because I usually stay somewhat removed from the community and I don't know many people."

"You're a recluse?" she teased with a smile so exciting he was tempted to kiss her again and damn the consequences.

"Not exactly a recluse. I go into town when I need supplies or services. Or when someone needs me. The truth is, when I worked for the FBI, I had my fill of all kinds of people. When I came back here, I just wanted peace and quiet."

Her pretty brows drew together as if she was trying again to decipher his motive. "A barn dance is *not* going to be peaceful or quiet."

Suddenly he realized that didn't bother him tonight. "No, it's not, but it'll give me a good chance to brush up on my manners and social skills," he joked, feeling in a lighter mood than he'd experienced since before his marriage had ended. Suddenly in spite of his doubts about bringing Gwen, he decided he was looking forward to the evening.

Laughing, Gwen stepped down from the SUV, her hand small in his.

He reluctantly released it.

After he locked the vehicle, they strolled toward the huge red barn. A floodlight glowed over the wide double doors. Juniper and spruce grew around the foundation. Clumps of people stood outside and the twangy sound of a band tuning up soared from the interior.

Garrett found himself taking Gwen's elbow over the uneven ground. To keep her safe or to simply touch her again? When she looked up at him, he muttered, "I don't want you to trip or turn an ankle."

The fringe of her shawl brushed over his hand, and her skin was warm under his fingertips. Breathing in her perfume, that fruity and floral mix, an erection pressed against his fly. Damn.

When they reached the gravel path leading to the barn, he dropped his hand. As long as they just do-si-doed and didn't get too close, his self-control would work just fine.

Gwen seemed to know everyone in Wild Horse Junction. Every two feet, somebody stopped her to say hello.

"You must get around," he murmured close to her ear as they wound around a few hay bales stacked for lounging and pure atmosphere.

"Get around?" Her brown eyes were soft and puzzled as she stopped to face him.

"You know everybody."

With a small shrug, she smiled. "That comes from

dealing with pregnant women. I meet their husbands and their families. If I help deliver a baby, they always introduce me to all their relatives."

"How many patients do you see in a week?"

"Fifty, maybe. It depends. Some weeks I do more home health care than others, and then I'm not in the office as much."

"Do you like what you do?"

"I love it. I help bring life into this world. What better job could I have?"

Gwen's optimistic outlook intrigued him. Where had she gotten it? With all he knew about her background, she had every excuse to see her glass half-empty. Yet she seemed genuinely satisfied with her life.

Tables were set up around the periphery of the barn with folding chairs. A wide open area had been left in front of the stage where the dancing would take place.

"Maybe we should grab a spot at a table before it gets too crowded," he decided.

They threaded their way along a row of tables. Suddenly a man stood and waved at them.

"It's my father." Gwen sounded surprised.

As they walked toward him, Garrett couldn't tell if she was happy to see her dad or not.

"We meet again," Russ said to Garrett. "You sure do look pretty, honey."

"Thanks, Dad. I didn't know you were coming."

"I was talking to Dorothy Otis at the post office—you know, she's the postal clerk there. Anyway, we both decided we could use a night out. She's supposed to meet me here."

"We won't butt in then," Gwen assured him quickly. "There are still plenty of seats at other tables."

"Don't be silly. I've got a chair for her and there's two more here. Get yourselves some cider and cookies and join me."

Gwen looked uncomfortable and Garrett had the feeling she didn't want to sit with her father. There was definitely a strain between father and daughter, mostly on the daughter's part.

She was looking up at him now. "Do you mind if we sit here?"

"One place is as good as another."

As Garrett pulled out a chair for Gwen, she glanced across the barn at the snack tables. Sliding her shawl from her shoulders, she folded it over a chair. "You go ahead and settle in. I'll get us a plate of cookies and whatever else I can find." Then she was on her way, disappearing into the crowds of people, waylaid almost immediately by a young pregnant woman.

"Have you known my daughter long?" Russ asked Garrett.

"Just a week. We're working on that case together."

"I thought maybe she asked you to help her because she'd known you for a while."

"I think she found me in the Yellow Pages," Garrett joked.

"I heard you own your own plane—a Cessna Skyhawk. Is that true?"

Garrett had the feeling Russ had been trying to find out more about him since they'd met at Gwen's. "It was my dad's."

"How did you lose him?" Russ asked.

"Pancreatic cancer." The disease had taken his dad fast, much faster than Garrett had ever expected. He wished he'd gone to L.A. to spend more time with him. But there had been work…and Cheryl. As it was, he'd gotten there just in time…just in time to say a last goodbye.

Conversations ebbed and flowed around them as Russ let Garrett alone with his thoughts for a few moments. Then he said, "I did some flying in the service—in Nam."

"Tell me about it," Garrett encouraged, wanting to find out more about this man who'd played a crucial role in Gwen's upbringing.

As Garrett listened to some of Russ's experiences, he realized he liked Gwen's dad, who in some ways reminded him of his own father. Glancing at his watch, he saw they'd been talking about twenty minutes and Gwen still hadn't returned to the table.

"The band is about ready to start," Garrett remarked, nodding toward the stage. "I'm going to see if I can find your daughter."

"I'm hoping my date will get here pretty soon, too. It's been a long time since I danced with a woman. I'm going to enjoy this."

If Garrett didn't corral Gwen, he had a feeling one person after another would monopolize her for the rest of the night.

A few minutes later, he spotted her at the food table and joined her there. "I thought you got lost."

"You and Dad seemed to be engrossed in conversation."

"He was talking about Vietnam."

"Dad *never* talks about Vietnam."

Garrett shrugged, "Maybe just not to you. Since he flew and I fly—"

Gwen gave him a smile that was strained. "It's nice to find common ground."

Since he was used to sincerity from Gwen, he knew he wasn't getting it now. Taking the plate of cookies from her hand, he set it on the table, took her arm and pulled her behind a stack of hay bales.

"What are we doing *here?*" she asked with a forced smile.

"If you and your dad are at odds, I don't want to step into something I have no right to step into."

"We're not at odds. In spite of myself and knowing I shouldn't, I want to help him too much. I want to ask if he's still attending meetings…regularly speaking with his sponsor…exercising…eating right."

Knowing he probably shouldn't interfere, he did, anyway. "I know Vietnam left deep wounds in lots of vets. Could he have post-traumatic stress and flash-backs that added to the drinking problem?"

This time she wasn't so quick to answer. "I don't think so," she admitted. "But then—" With a sigh, she said in a low voice, "Maybe my mother leaving was a trigger. I never thought about it that way. I knew after she left, I had to take over everything—from cooking to balancing the checkbook as soon as I was old enough to worry about bills. I took care of Dad when he couldn't take care of himself. I made sure we had groceries. He managed to work on and off and kept a roof over our heads. But bills stacked up. We'd lose electricity or the telephone. I thought I was helping him by doing things for him. When I was at college, I felt guilty for feeling free. Yet I went home often to make sure he was functioning. And he was to a certain extent. After I graduated, I lived with him because I thought he needed looking after. One weekend he binged and didn't come home for three days. That's when I went to counseling and an Al-Anon meeting."

Garrett saw the sheen of tears in her eyes as she blinked fast. "On the advice of my counselor, I practiced tough love with him. Nothing in my life has ever been so hard. I told him if he was going to drink himself into a grave, I wasn't going to be around to watch."

Bravery took many forms and Garrett realized just how brave this woman had been. "Since he's alive and well, tough love must have worked."

"I think it did. I hope it did. But when I don't hear from him for a day or two, I'm afraid he's slipped back."

The band started playing and Garrett had to bend his head low to hers so she could hear him. "There's an old adage, what we fear, we create."

"Because I'm afraid he'll fall off the wagon, he will? Apparently you've never lived with an alcoholic." The tears were gone now and she looked angry.

She would have walked away from him, but he found he couldn't let her. Catching her hand, he pulled her back to their private corner. "I'm sorry if I sounded…patronizing. I didn't mean it to come out that way. Yet if you're watching him every second for signs of a fall, don't you think he can feel that? Don't you think that makes him wonder, too?"

When she didn't respond yet didn't move away, he

nodded to where the folks were gathering to dance. "Come on. Two-step with me."

She studied him intently for a few moments and he knew she was trying to gauge what kind of man he was. If his ex-wife could answer that question, she'd tell Gwen he was a selfish SOB who'd put his job before his family. But Gwen must have seen something different, or maybe just decided dancing was better than talking.

With a half smile, she responded, "I'd like that."

The space cleared for dancing was crowded with couples who knew how to two-step. Gwen wasn't prepared for the heady, climb-to-the-mountaintop sensations that overwhelmed her as Garrett took her into his arms. This man rattled her but he also unlocked deep, womanly feelings she had kept in a sealed cache since she was left alone at the church to explain Mark's desertion to their wedding guests. On the other hand, maybe she'd sealed that cache long before that.

Although she tried to concentrate on the steps, rather than Garrett's hard, tall body, his muscled arms, the scent of lime aftershave, she found herself way too distracted to keep her feet in step. Once she almost tripped but he caught her, twirled her in a circle and resumed the pattern of the two-step.

"You're good," she breathed.

Nothing seemed to unnerve him. His eyes were deep gray and there was a sensual storm building there that had to do with a man and woman dancing, attracted to each other, yet trying to deny chemistry that was definitely there.

They danced one dance after another, Garrett leading

her in more intricate steps each time, adding more twirls. He had a natural rhythm she envied. They didn't talk and she found herself breathless, not from the dancing, but from him.

"Would you like to take a break?" he asked her after they participated in a round of square dancing. Do-si-do with Garrett gave new meaning to the term.

"It is getting hot in here," she said, fanning herself with her hand and pushing her hair behind her ear.

With that slow enigmatic smile of his that made her knees wobble, he beckoned her to follow him. Heading to the rear of the barn, opposite the entrance where they'd come in, he led her through a side door.

"Do you need your shawl?" he asked as a breeze brushed them.

"I'm fine," she replied although the cool end of September night air gave her chills. She shivered.

"Why do women say they're fine when they're not?" he muttered, and she had to laugh.

"You've had experience with that?"

"Way too much. Come on." Leading her away from the flood lights and the music and the chatter, he headed toward a smaller barn. Lifting the latch, he opened the door.

"Won't Mr. Wilkins mind if we go in here?"

"No."

"Do you know Ted Wilkins?" She was beginning to see Garrett didn't give information unless she prodded him for it.

"His son sold me my log home, so Ted knows I won't steal his horses."

There were six stalls and three of them were filled.

A bay softly neighed, welcoming them. A yellow tabby suddenly appeared at Gwen's feet and wrapped itself around her legs. Smiling, she stooped and picked it up. The cat purred as she rubbed it under the chin. It looked young if size were an indication. Not a kitten, but not yet an adult.

"I thought about getting a cat," she mused.

"Why haven't you?"

"Because I'm away from the house so much. It just doesn't seem fair to have a pet and not spend time with it."

"Cats are independent, at least that's what I've heard."

"Even independent creatures need someone to pet them and love them and just sit with them."

"Are you speaking from experience?"

Her attention drawn from the cat with his words, she looked up and wished she hadn't. He saw entirely too much.

Lowering the tabby to the floor, she protested, "I wasn't projecting."

"No?"

His raised brows irritated her. "No. I'm perfectly content with my life."

"You don't need someone to pet you and keep you company?" His voice was low and seductive and she found herself being honest with him.

"Sometimes I wish I had someone to hold me at night."

"Just hold you?"

When he brought his hand to her face, she couldn't look away. She couldn't move. She could only feel the excitement stirred up by being around him.

His calloused thumb traced her cheekbone. "You are one beautiful woman."

Had anyone told her she was beautiful before?

The cynic in her made her wonder if Garrett was feeding her flattery. Yet what she already knew about him told her he wasn't that type of man. She felt herself sinking into his gray eyes, allowed her body to hum with the anticipation vibrating between them, saw hunger that frightened her yet challenged her. Garrett Maxwell raised so much curiosity inside of her that she almost keened with it. Would his lips be hot? Would his tongue be rough? Would his kiss be ordinary this time or extraordinary like their first? Could he turn on the tap of passion she'd only ever dreamed about but never experienced?

Garrett cupped her face in both of his large calloused hands, tipped her chin up and murmured, "I've dreamed of doing this again."

The fact that this attraction definitely wasn't one-sided almost made her grin. But then his lips captured hers and the roller-coaster sensation she always felt with him excited her until she lost all sense of time and place. There was more raw need in Garrett's kiss than finesse. It took less than a moment for his lips to part, for his tongue to slip into her mouth. Not only were his lips hot, but his tongue was erotically talented. Every spot it found seemed vulnerable, and she lifted her arms around his neck and pressed closer to him. When her breasts pushed against his chest, he groaned, slid his hands down her back and pressed her tighter to him.

Kisses usually escalated in steps from slow to fast,

from simple to complex, from hunger and desire to full-blown need. With this kiss, she could almost feel the whoosh as they bypassed the beginning of easy and simple and headed straight for the heart of the fire.

Where did a kiss go from here?

Garrett didn't seem to have any problem figuring that out. His lower body against hers told her exactly where he was going. The heck of it was she wanted to follow him, even if just for a little while.

There was a hush in the barn that was as intimate as a bedroom. Country music floated in the distance as an owl hooted, but the sound fit in rather than jarred her. She was even more aware of her heart pounding along with Garrett's. Excitement building between them, his hands dipped down to her backside and before she knew what he was about, he was gathering her skirt and lifting it. She'd worn panty hose tonight but nothing seemed to deter him as his hands slipped inside her panties and cupped her. She thought she'd explode. His caresses were so intimate…so personal…so knowing.

Yet he didn't know her and she didn't know him. What in the blue blazes was she doing? The rate this was going, their clothes soon would be on the floor and they'd be rolling in the hay.

How did she get out of this one with her dignity intact?

First she stopped responding to his kiss, then she arched her body, putting a little space between them.

That's all it took. Apparently Garrett was the type of man who knew how to read signals. He could tell she was shutting down.

He pulled his hands free and let her skirt fall. When

she looked at him, he wore an expression she couldn't decipher. She had a feeling he was practiced at the neutral look, and it had been a tool of his work. She guessed he'd used it often in his personal life, too.

She told herself again, she didn't really know him.

"Should I apologize for that?" he asked gruffly, the only indication they'd been doing something other than talking.

"Do you want to?"

After studying her, he smiled. "Hell, no." Then his smile slipped away. "But you're not the type of woman who would enjoy a quickie in the barn, are you?"

She wasn't exactly sure what to say to that. "I didn't think so before tonight. Do you do this..." she waved at where they were standing "...often?"

"Since my divorce, I've been more celibate than satisfied. And I have to be honest with you, Gwen, there's a reason for that. I don't intend to take on the responsibility of marriage ever again. I don't believe in the illusion of forever vows. Forever doesn't exist for me. And I have a feeling you're still looking for it. That's probably why this shouldn't happen again."

"Maybe you're wrong."

"A quickie in a barn is fine with you? No regrets afterward? No dreams of wedding veils or honeymoons?"

Her answer must have shown on her face.

"You're transparent, Gwen."

Angry now as well as defensive, she responded, "And you've got a monumental ego. I've known you about five minutes. Why would I be thinking about a wedding veil? Or even a romp in the hay with you?"

He tapped her nose. "I was speaking hypothetically. Let's go back to the square dancing and work off some of this energy."

"Only if we dance in different squares," she grumbled.

At that, Garrett Maxwell gave a hearty laugh. He was laughing at her and she didn't like it one bit.

When Garrett saw Gwen rocking little Amy in the hospital nursery the following Thursday, he felt as if he'd been poleaxed. Something about the picture made his breaths come hard and his chest tighten.

What had happened Saturday night in the barn should have kept him away from here…and away from Gwen. Yet she was the one who had started him on this search. She was the one who in some sense of the word, had "hired" him. She deserved to know what he'd found and what he was going to do next.

Gwen spied him through the window and gave him a "just a minute" sign.

Checking his watch, he knew her lunch hour was about over and she'd have to leave the hospital soon.

When Gwen stood, cuddling Amy in her arms, Garrett turned away. He'd given up on the idea of having kids. In his book that would require a wife. And what did he know about being a good husband? His own dad had been a poor role model. As a pilot, he'd hardly ever been home, and Garrett suspected more than flying an aircraft went on when he was gone. He'd heard his parents arguing. He'd heard his mother's pleas for his father to settle down, open his own air cargo company so he could stay local. His father, at those times, had told Garrett's mom he'd think about it, but he never had. His lifestyle had suited him and he hadn't wanted to change it.

Garrett had seen that. Maybe he'd been taught a man's career *should* come first. When he'd met Cheryl, he hadn't given a second thought to what he did for a living. After all, he'd been an agent for five years when he'd met her, and the idea his job would be a problem had never even crossed his mind. It hadn't seemed to bother her, either, until after they were married…until he got work-related calls in the middle of the night and on weekends…until she decided she wanted a baby.

He glanced back over his shoulder into the nursery and was sorry he did. Gwen was leaning down into the little crib, placing a kiss on the baby's forehead.

Damn, he shouldn't be here. He should have told Gwen he couldn't take her case. He should have dropped this whole situation like a hot poker.

When Gwen stepped out of the nursery, he could see she didn't know whether to smile or frown at him. After their make-out session in the barn, they'd joined separate squares to dance. On their way home, conversation had been awkward, what little there had been of it.

"I called your cell phone, but got your voice mail," he said in explanation of why he was here.

"I can't have it on in the hospital. What's happened?"

"I have the names of the women who bought the yarn in the shop in Laramie. I'm going to fly there tomorrow."

"I want to go with you."

"Gwen, there's no reason for you to go with me."

"There's every reason for me to go with you. Amy's

going into foster care tomorrow. This is probably the last time I'll hold her. I want her mother found."

"You don't think I can do that? Isn't that why you hired me?"

Instead of answering that directly, she returned with, "Aren't two sets of eyes and ears better than one? And maybe being back in Laramie, my memory will become clearer about the young girls I talked to there."

"That's a long shot."

"Maybe it is, but it's one I feel I have to take." Then she squared her shoulders and defiantly looked up at him. "Is there some reason you don't want me to go with you? Maybe your plane only holds one person?"

Gwen's feisty assertiveness sometimes made him want to shake her, sometimes made him laugh, sometimes simply frustrated him. "You'll fit in the plane."

Unbidden thoughts of last night nudged him. He'd awakened in a hot sweat because of a dream he'd had of the two of them rolling around in a hay loft.

"You can just take off tomorrow?" he asked.

"This is important, Garrett. I'll do what I have to do. If I have to see double my patients on Monday, I will."

He had to admire her determination as well as her motivation, but he knew her own history was driving her as much as her worry over little Amy.

"You can't right what happened when you were a kid." As soon as the words were out of his mouth, he was reminded that he'd been trying to do the same thing since his friend had been kidnapped when he was nine.

"I'm not trying to do that."

"Aren't you? I don't know what you think happened

with Amy, but apparently her mother didn't want her. She left her. End of story."

"That's *not* the end of the story and you know it," Gwen protested heatedly. "Why did she leave her? Did she *want* to leave her? Does she need support? Does she have any family? If she is a teenager and just had a baby? She might not even be making rational decisions. Don't give me that end-of-story line."

"You want there to be a reason why *your* mother left *you.*"

After a taut moment of silence, she nodded. "Of course, I do. I know there *was,* but I'll never know *what* it was. Don't you see? I need to prevent that from happening to Amy. I know what it's done to me. I know my background is the reason my heart's in this. Is there something wrong with that?"

If his life was any indication, he shouldn't see anything wrong with it. She was using her sadness to try to improve a situation. Isn't that what he did every time he searched for a lost child? He'd lost a friend, he'd lost his marriage and he'd lost a baby. Was he trying to make up for all of that by reuniting kids with their parents?

Damn straight, he was.

"All right, we'll leave around 8:00 a.m., weather permitting. Can you meet me at the hangar?"

"Sure. Is there anything in particular I should bring along?"

"In case we crash, survive and have to live in the wilds of Wyoming for a week?"

"You have a terrific sense of melodrama," she complained. "You should have been a script writer. No, I was thinking about lunch."

Garrett couldn't help the laugh that escaped him. For whatever else Gwen was, she was a match for him and he liked that.

"I'll spring for lunch when we get to Laramie."

Gwen checked her watch. "I have to go. I have a home visit and I don't want to be late." Then she gazed at him with wide brown eyes. "We *are* going to find this mother, aren't we?"

"We're going to do our best."

As he walked with Gwen to the nurses' desk, he knew that in the past his best hadn't always been good enough.

This time, however, in his gut, he knew his best was going to find this mother. He also understood that Gwen wasn't going to let him do it alone.

Chapter Five

"You drove all the way from Wild Horse Junction to ask me what I knitted with my yarn? Haven't you heard of that modern invention called the telephone?" Bonnie Treadway asked, as Gwen and Garrett sat in her lace-curtained living room.

A petite woman, dressed in jeans and a plaid blouse with short cropped gray hair, she looked like someone's energetic grandmother, Gwen thought as she studied her.

They hadn't flown to Laramie after all. Storm cells had moved in so Garrett decided to drive.

"As I explained," Garrett said, "I'm investigating a case and personally tracking down every lead I can find. I learned of only three customers who bought that yarn from the Bows and Baskets craft shop. It was the first time she'd ordered it because it was expensive. One of the women hasn't knitted anything with hers yet, another used hers for insets in an afghan. Can you tell us what you did with yours?"

Bonnie smiled. "Of course I can, but I don't see how it will help. It comes in those little skeins, and Flo only had three of them left when I bought it on sale. I barely had enough to make a baby sweater and hat."

Garrett followed up with, "Did you give them to anyone special?"

There was absolutely no hesitation when Bonnie answered and Gwen knew she had nothing to hide…and no one to protect.

"Sure, I gave it to the Thrift Store. I often make sweaters and little hats and donate them. It's my way of contributing to charity. I can't do much else on Social Security. It was a treat finding that yarn at a price I could afford."

When Garrett exchanged a look with Gwen, she knew what he was thinking. This might be like looking for a needle in a haystack. Then again, Laramie was a town of about thirty thousand. There were loads of specialty shops behind quaint Victorian facades that were geared at tourists. But this time of year, tourists dwindled off, and locals were more likely to shop at the Thrift Store. They could get lucky.

"Where is this thrift shop located?"

"It's over on South Second Street by the Children's Museum. You can't miss it. There's a bright green awning with Thrift Store stenciled on it. It's not open on Fridays, though."

"Not open?" Gwen thought Friday would be a high traffic day.

"Nope. It's hard for Flo to get help on Fridays, and she's gone all day. She takes turns with her sisters sitting with her mother. Friday is her day. She should be open tomorrow. She's listed in the phone book under F. Wiggins. She's a widow, too."

"You've been helpful, Mrs. Treadway," Garrett said, standing now. "Thank you for answering our questions."

"Can you tell me what this is all about? What kind of case are you working on?"

After Garrett debated a second or two, he answered, "A baby was abandoned. She was wearing a sweater and hat made with yarn like you bought. We're trying to track down the mother or maybe some family."

"Goodness. And you think it might be my sweater and hat on that baby? Well, I wish you luck. Would you like some tea before you go? Maybe some cookies?"

Garrett shook his head. "No, we're fine. We'll probably stop at that bed-and-breakfast we passed coming in. Is it a good one?"

"The Lantern Inn? The blue house with the white trim?" Bonnie asked.

Garrett nodded.

"That's Cora and Abe Martin's place. Yes, it's wonderful. She serves the best breakfast in town and provides lunches, too. I think she has five rooms. This time of year, you'll probably be able to get one…or maybe even two." She looked quizzically at Garrett and back to Gwen.

Although Bonnie Treadway was nice, Gwen wasn't

about to give her the details of her personal life. She also didn't know if she liked the idea of staying overnight there with Garrett. Something about a bed-and-break-fast seemed a little too cozy.

After they said their goodbyes to Bonnie and thanked her again, they walked to Garrett's SUV. Once inside, Gwen thought about the drive to Laramie. There'd been small talk for a while, but that had soon ebbed away and Garrett had switched on the CD player. They'd made good time. It had taken about four hours. During the entire drive, Gwen had been supersensitive to every-thing about Garrett, from the scent of his aftershave to the movement of his leg on the accelerator and brake, his large hands on the steering wheel, his glances her way every now and then.

Once in the car now, Garrett reached to the backseat, picking up a Laramie phone book. Quickly he paged through it. Phone in hand, he punched in the number for Flo Wiggins. "If no one answers, do you have a problem staying here overnight?"

It was nice of him to ask after he'd already made up his mind. "And if I said I did?"

"Is this a financial dilemma or a personal one?"

What an interesting way to put it! "I can spring for a room for tonight. Why a bed-and-breakfast rather than two motel rooms?" She didn't emphasize the *two,* but he got the gist.

"I want you to be safe. Bed-and-breakfasts are usu-ally a little more secure. They have an investment to protect. Plus they're usually a bit more comfortable."

She couldn't argue with him, because she felt the

same way. Often when she traveled, she searched out B-and-Bs rather than staying in a motel. "I should let my dad know I'm out of town. I don't want him to try to get hold of me and worry. Saturday morning he often calls to see if I want to go for breakfast."

"And do you?"

"Sure. I can see how he's doing that way."

Garrett's brows arched. "Meaning you can check up on him."

"I've separated my life from his now," she assured him softly.

"Gwen, you do realize *you* weren't the reason he drank?"

His question made her breath catch. When she was a kid, she'd blamed herself. But as an adult… "My adopted mother was the reason he drank, but I *let* him drink."

Emphatically, Garrett shook his head. "You were a kid. My guess is, once he was into drinking a couple of years, he didn't even remember *why* he was drinking— your mom, Nam, the responsibility of raising a child alone. You get so used to numbing the pain, you just don't want to feel anything."

All of Gwen's annoyance at Garrett's know-best attitude went quiet. "You sound as if you know."

Silence filled the SUV. Drizzle from the gray clouds dripped down the windshield.

After a few moments, Garrett responded, "I've never used alcohol to drown my sorrows if that's what you mean, but in the work I did, I had to turn off my emotions. I had to think like a computer at times—no heart. When a man does that, sometimes he can't turn it back on again."

"You mean like…with your wife."

This time she really thought he wouldn't reply, but then he answered, "Yes, with my wife."

Tossing the phone book into the backseat, he cut off their conversation. "Let's see if the Lantern Inn has two rooms."

The Martins, who were a couple in their late forties, welcomed Gwen and Garrett to their B-and-B. A fire was blazing in the parlor where the reservation desk was located and Garrett noticed the bottle of wine and cookies set out for guests. There were also insulated decanters of coffee and hot water for tea. The parlor seemed to be scented with something and he noticed a dish of potpourri sitting on an occasional table.

"This is beautiful," Gwen said, looking up at the crown molding around the ceiling.

Mrs. Martin smiled. "It's been in Abe's family for three generations."

Figuring the women could easily become embroiled in a conversation about the history of the house, the fabric on the chairs…anything…Garrett got to the point. "Do you have any vacancies for tonight? We need two rooms."

He was still a bit unnerved by what he'd said to Gwen about his marriage. He didn't know where it had come from, just that it had been lurking in his mind for a long time. He didn't empty his soul so easily and he felt that's what he'd done.

"Why, yes, we have vacancies," Mrs. Martin told him with a nod. "We even have two rooms, but they connect with a shared bathroom. Would they suit?"

Connecting with a shared bathroom. Temptation—a hop, skip and a jump away. Not exactly what he had in mind. It looked like a nice place, though. He'd seen the hefty lock on the door and the panel for the security system. He wasn't an expert, but most of the furniture looked like antiques.

His gaze locked to Gwen's. "Do you have a problem with connecting rooms?"

He supposed he could have pulled her into the hall for this conversation, yet the Martins still could have overheard.

"Do both rooms have doors leading into the bathroom?" Gwen asked.

"Why, yes, they do."

To Garrett she replied, "I don't have a problem."

However, he saw a flicker in her eyes. Anxiety? Anticipation? He wasn't sure.

"Wonderful," Mrs. Martin exclaimed.

Her husband added, "We just need a credit card."

While Gwen reached into her purse, Garrett pulled out his wallet.

Her hand covered his. "Let me take care of this." She lowered her voice. "You're doing this for me."

Gwen's fingers on his hand created all sorts of electric signals shooting to his brain, letting desire escape from the box where he'd kept it dormant all day.

The Martins were watching them with interest and he didn't want to cause a scene. He also knew Gwen's pride was important to her just as his was important to him.

"All right," he decided, pulling away from her touch, pulling away from feelings that had been bub-

bling up since he'd met Gwen. He'd had them stowed
away for so long....

"If you folks would like a light supper, we can bring
it to your rooms. We have roast beef sandwiches, a fresh
vegetable dish, my own potato salad and peanut butter
pie for dessert."

With a glance out the window, Garrett could see the
rain was heavier now. "That sounds good to me." When
he checked with Gwen, she nodded.

Minutes later, they were following Mrs. Martin up
two flights of stairs to the third floor. Both rooms, one
decorated in lilac-flowered chintz, the other in blue,
had slanted ceilings. The rain pattered on the roof.

When the hostess left them, Gwen could feel the
intimacy of the space. It felt as if the two of them were
on top of the world...alone. Nervously, she moved into
the bathroom with its large shower, double vanity and
other accoutrements. There was even a warming rack
for towels.

"Blue room or purple one?" Garrett asked her.

"The purple one," Gwen decided. "This place really
is charming. They seem like nice people."

Standing in the bathroom with Garrett, Gwen felt the
familiarity of it. She was alone with a strange man in
rooms practically secluded from the rest of the house.

"Are you really all right with this?" he asked her, obviously sensing some of her concern.

She wrapped her arms around herself as though she
was chilled. She wasn't afraid of him. It was just...the
situation was unusual.

Unexpectedly he reached out, putting his hands on her

shoulders. "You can trust me, Gwen. You're safe with me. If this isn't comfortable for you, we can find a motel."

When she looked into his eyes, she couldn't tell what he was thinking. Yet she didn't have to read his thoughts to know she could trust him. Ever since Mark had left her waiting with her dad in the vestibule of the church, she had wondered about her judgment, especially concerning men. Instinct told her Garrett could be trusted. But were her instincts right or skewed by the attraction between them?

"Our doors lock," he added gruffly.

"Yes, I know they do. I'll be fine. This is fine."

"Good. I think I'll get a shower," he decided, looking relieved. "What are you going to do?"

"I'll call Dad. And I'll try to call Flo once again. If I get hold of her, maybe she wouldn't mind a visit tonight."

He was still clasping her shoulders and she knew she should move away.

He didn't seem eager to cut off their contact, either. "I want to kiss you again, but I think we decided that wouldn't be a good idea."

Maybe he was waiting for consent from her, for her to tell him she'd changed almost overnight to a woman who would go for a quickie in a bed-and-breakfast, if not a barn, with a man she still didn't know very well. She did want to feel Garrett's lips on hers. She almost ached to have his touch on her skin again. Yet she hadn't changed. She always looked at consequences before she leaped. Making love with Garrett was a leap that could land her into a very deep ravine.

"I'll go make those calls."

He dropped his hands and stepped away. He wouldn't push or coax or persuade. She knew he wasn't that kind of man.

Leaving the bathroom, she closed her door and leaned against it, breathing hard as if she'd just run a race.

After Gwen called her dad and left a message, she tried Flo Wiggins's number again and got no answer. She paced the room. She needed a toothbrush and toothpaste. She needed a book to read. She needed something to distract her from being up here with Garrett.

The water was running now in the shower and she thought about him naked, standing there, letting the water sluice on his face, his chest, his...

Blowing out a breath, she grabbed her jacket and hurried to the stairs. There was a drugstore kitty-corner from the inn. She could find everything she needed there. Maybe she'd even pick up a razor for Garrett. Beard stubble on his strong jaw would only make him look sexier. He was already sexy enough!

After Garrett finished showering, he toweled off, stepped into his jeans without underwear. He thought about Gwen just behind that closed door. Staying overnight here had been a stupid idea. If they'd gone to a motel and he'd worried about her safety, he could have sat in the car outside her door.

Thinking about stepping into a cold shower again, he carefully zipped his jeans. Usually he kept a duffel of extra clothes in his SUV, but this trip he'd been distracted. He was definitely losing his edge.

Because of the woman?

He almost guffawed at that.

After he went to his bedroom, he looked at his shirt. He could just leave it off, but they had to get through dinner together, yet, and the way his mind had been racing, he'd be imagining her lips and her hands on him.

Disgusted with himself, he shrugged into the shirt and buttoned it quickly, not bothering to tuck it in. A few minutes later, after donning socks and boots, he stood at the door to Gwen's room and rapped.

When she didn't answer, he frowned. Maybe she'd fallen asleep.

Calling her name, he opened the door. She was nowhere to be found. That seemed odd. He stepped into the hall, his heart beating faster. Maybe she'd gone downstairs to talk to Mrs. Martin.

But after inquiring if the hostess had seen Gwen, he found out she hadn't and worry tangled his insides. After checking outside, he found Gwen was nowhere around the SUV. And why would she be? She didn't have a key.

Frustrated and unsettled, he went back to his room and paced.

Is this the way Cheryl had felt when she didn't know where he was or what he was doing? When he had to drop out of sight for a few days? When he landed an undercover assignment that had taken him away for a couple of weeks?

And what about when she was pregnant? She'd begged him not to take that last assignment. The doctor had told him worry alone couldn't cause a miscarriage, but Garrett was as sure now as he was then that it had played a part. He had caused her miscarriage—*their* miscarriage—the loss of their baby.

When he heard the clatter of shoes on the stairs, he went still. Not waiting for Gwen to enter her room, he met her in the hall.

"Where have you been?" he growled.

It took him a few moments to observe the fact that she was dripping wet and so was the newspaper she'd tried to hold over her head to protect her from the rain.

Holding two bags in her other hand, she smiled. "I just went to get supplies. You know women, can't stay overnight someplace without shampoo and—" She stopped. "What's wrong?"

He stuffed his hands into his jeans pockets. "Nothing's wrong. I just didn't know where you were."

"What did you think? That I'd vanished into thin air? You were getting your shower, and I certainly wasn't going to try to communicate through a shower door."

"You could have left a note." Then before she could see how rattled he'd really been, he went into his room.

Instead of going to hers, however, she followed him. "I knew I was only going to be gone a few minutes." Her curls were wet and curling more than usual above her jacket collar.

"You're dripping on the floor," he pointed out. "You'd better get dried off."

After setting the newspaper and the bags on a wooden chair, she moved closer to him. The rain seemed to enhance the scent of her perfume or shampoo or whatever it was that had driven him crazy all day in the car.

"I didn't mean to worry you," she said softly.

He wasn't going to deny that she had. "Forget it. Go get changed."

"I take care of myself, Garrett. I'm not used to announcing my comings and goings, even when I lived with Dad. He didn't usually know if I was there or if I wasn't, and he really didn't care."

"Because of the alcohol," Garrett said gruffly.

"Yes. Were you truly worried? What did you think might have happened?"

His defenses felt as thin as a veil around this woman. "We're in a strange town. Who knows? When you've seen what I've seen—women getting snatched, kids getting snatched, men who don't have a conscience, you learn nowhere's safe. Even in the best of circumstances, life's a crap shoot."

"What kind of work did you do?"

"I did whatever was asked of me."

Her voice went even softer. "And what did it cost you?"

"It cost me my marriage and a child."

Her eyes went wide. "Someone took your child?"

"No. This wasn't the fault of a bad guy. I was the bad guy."

Her hands fluttered out as if to touch his arm in comfort, but he couldn't let her do that. He crossed to the window and stared out at the rain. "Cheryl knew I was FBI when she married me. I think she was impressed by the idea—that it was glamorous or something. I don't know."

"Dangerous men can be the most sexy," Gwen murmured.

He glanced at her and saw that she meant it. "*I* wasn't

dangerous, but my job could be and I couldn't talk about most of it. I don't know what Cheryl thought. That I'd sit behind a desk, in a suit, carry a gun, arrest perps from a distance."

"What did you do?"

"It wasn't only what I did, but how and when I did it. Cheryl began to resent the beep of my cell phone, a call to duty in the middle of the night, situations that sometimes kept me away for days."

"Was not understanding your work the biggest problem?"

"Yes, or else our personalities were…or our expectations. I'm still not sure. Cheryl expected marriage to be a forever love fest, but then the realities of life set in."

"Neither of you got what you bargained for."

"*That* is the ultimate understatement. After she became pregnant, I talked to my supervisor. I was assigned to cases close to home."

Gwen was near again, and he hadn't heard her move. "Where was home?" she asked.

"Northern Virginia." The sound of the rain drowned out his heartbeat, a beat that grew harder and stronger around Gwen.

"What happened?"

There didn't seem to be any turning back now. "I got involved in a case before Cheryl got pregnant. Details aren't important, but the information I had in my head was. Anyway, the long and short of it was that I was called away for a week. While I was gone, Cheryl miscarried."

When no sound came from Gwen, he swung to face her. He was surprised to see her eyes bright with tears.

The *rat-a-tat* of rain on the roof pounded in his ears until Gwen said, "She blamed you."

"We *both* blamed me. I put work before her and the baby."

Gwen didn't recoil or look away. "Could you have turned down the assignment?"

"No. Not 'no' as in I'd lose my job if I did, but 'no,' as in we had to round up someone who was going to hurt even more people if I did."

"She didn't understand the duty and responsibility of who you are?"

How did Gwen know him so well in such a short time? "She believed duty and responsibility to her and our child came first. Now I think she was right. I think it's hard for men to separate ego from their job."

"You think ego drove you rather than duty?"

He kept his gaze locked to hers and said honestly, "I'll never know."

After a moment, she asked, "Is that why you left the FBI?"

He blew out a breath, glad this discussion was almost over. "I didn't leave until after my divorce. I told Cheryl I'd quit and do something in security. But she'd given up on us."

"No counseling?"

"She said that wasn't in the cards. No counselor could make her forgive me."

Gwen's eyes went deeply brown as if she couldn't imagine saying that to someone. But *she* hadn't lost a child. *She* hadn't been on the other end of a marriage with a husband who disappeared for days and left at the beep of a cell phone. What kind of woman could forgive a man who did that to her?

What kind of woman could live with his lifestyle now, solitary most of the time before taking off at the sound of a cell phone to rescue a child?

The answer wasn't so elusive—the kind of woman who could understand just how important rescuing children was to him. The kind of woman who could love a man *more* that she needed him.

A bead of water dripped from Gwen's hair onto her jacket collar. She'd stood there listening to him as if she weren't wet all over.

"You've got to get changed," he said.

"Garrett…"

He held up his hands to stop the comfort she wanted to give, and almost touched her. But he closed his hands into a fist instead. "Enough. It does no good to rehash history."

"It does if you learn from it. It does if it helps you connect with someone else."

Connect. Damn if he didn't feel a connection to this woman, and he hadn't gone looking for it. He shouldn't have connected at all. She was optimism, he was cynicism. She was hopeful, he was pragmatic. She had dreams and his were long gone. What *did* connect them?

Her brown eyes pulled on the strings of the protective web around his heart. Her worry about Baby Amy urged him to help her. Her freckles, her curls, her smile, jump-started an engine that had run in neutral since long before his divorce.

"Staying here tonight wasn't a good idea," he admitted.

"It's cozier than a motel."

"It's too cozy. If you get out of those wet clothes, what are you going to put on?"

"I bought a sleep shirt at the drugstore."

The idea of a sleep shirt didn't seem a good alternative measure to Garrett. "And then I suppose you'll wrap a sheet around you for a robe?"

"I can," Gwen assured him with a solemn nod.

Garrett didn't know whether to laugh or shake her. "I'm going to regret bringing you along."

"Do you want to list the reasons why?"

"No, I don't. But I know you'll push until I do. So here goes. Number one, I don't need a sidekick. Number two, I eventually draw out the information I need. Number three, I don't like partnering with women, because there's too much chance of misunderstanding, more with regard to the case than personal matters. Men and women just don't think alike. Number four, the idea of you in a sleep shirt in a bed twenty feet away isn't my idea of investigating a case."

Straightening her spine, she also squared her shoulders. "I can eat alone."

"That might be a very good idea."

If he wanted to push her away, he'd succeeded because the look in her eyes said she was hurt as well as…disappointed?

Without another word, she picked up her bags and went into the bathroom, leaving drips on the hardwood floor. He heard the door close to her bedroom. It wasn't a slam, but it might as well have been.

They were done connecting…at least for tonight.

* * *

It was midnight when Garrett glanced at his luminous watch dial. He'd never minded silence. The on-and-off drip of rain usually put him to sleep. But after getting the frustration of being near Gwen and emotionally exposing himself off his chest, he felt like a heel.

Gwen hadn't changed into her sleep shirt, at least not until after Cora had brought supper to them and they'd gone to their separate rooms. Then he hadn't seen her again. After dinner, in a very polite voice, she'd announced through his door that she was going to get a shower. The problem was—he could hear the sounds from the bathroom all too well, and his imagination was too vivid for his own good. Not only that, but a steamy gardenia scent had seeped under the door and invaded his room in a continuous cloud that he'd finally had to escape. He'd gone downstairs to the parlor, had a glass of wine, chosen a magazine and sat there and read it cover to cover. When he returned upstairs, Gwen had been closeted in her own room again but the bathroom wasn't the same. The gardenia smell lingered. He noticed her toothbrush and toothpaste, shampoo, conditioner and lotions she'd obviously bought at the drugstore. Then on his side of the double sink, he caught sight of the disposable razor, another toothbrush and an extra-large white T-shirt. She'd thought about him on her shopping excursion.

He'd almost knocked on her door then. Almost.

Now he sat up on the edge of the bed. Yellow glow from a streetlamp seeped through the blinds so he didn't turn on a light, just grabbed his jeans from the chair next to the bed and slid them on.

When he opened his door into the bathroom, he saw light under her door. Secretly he'd hoped she'd be asleep and this could wait until morning.

"Gwen," he called. "Are you awake?"

Her voice sailed through the closed door. "I'm awake, but I'm in my sleep shirt and I don't have a sheet wrapped around me."

In spite of himself, he had to smile. That was the thing about Gwen Langworthy. Her dry humor whetted his appetite for more. There hadn't been any laughter in his life for a long time.

"Can I come in anyway?"

There was only a brief hesitation until she answered, "Come on in."

Gwen wasn't wrapped in a sheet, but she *was* in bed with the covers drawn up over her breasts. There was a slight wariness in her eyes but it was replaced by something else that lit a fuse in him as her gaze settled on his chest, on his navel, and traveled back up to his face.

"Can't sleep?" she asked lightly, setting aside the magazine she was reading.

"No, I can't. I shouldn't have been so harsh earlier."

"You weren't harsh, you were just stating the situation as you saw it."

"No, what I was trying to do was to build a solid wall between us."

Surprise flickered over her face that he'd admitted his motives.

"We're attracted to each other, Gwen. That's been

obvious since we set sight on each other. But I don't intend to foul up your life or let you complicate mine."

"You have to put yourself in a position of power, don't you?" she asked softly.

Anger rose up fast and furious. "It has nothing to do with power or control. I'm looking out for both of us."

She scooted over on the bed under the covers, then she patted the quilt.

Gwen was a communicator. God save men from women who wanted to talk! If she'd invited him into her bed to have sex, he could have turned her down flat because he knew it was best for both of them. However, he couldn't turn down this invitation to communicate, not after what he'd said to her earlier. With patience born of years in the field—he was going to listen and not talk himself—he sat by her hip, inhaling the scent of gardenias.

"You're not my protector. You've no right to make decisions for me," she began. "If you don't want to get involved, if you want to back away, that's fine. But don't base your actions on what you think is best for me or what you think I want, not unless you ask me." There wasn't any anger in her words, just maybe a hint of exasperation.

"I'm used to being in charge," he admitted, seeing what she meant about wanting power and control.

"But you've also worked on teams, I imagine. You do that when you try to rescue a child. Don't you think of us as a team?"

He wanted to deny there was an "us" but if he looked

at the two of them honestly, he couldn't do that. "You're too smart for your own good," he grumbled.

"You don't like smart women?"

"I like smart women. But not when kissing them rattles my bones."

She was looking at him as if the kiss and thinking about it rattled her bones, too. If he kissed her now, she'd soon lose that sleep shirt and his jeans would be on the floor before he could say her name.

Standing, he informed her, "We'll get breakfast in the morning and then go to that thrift shop."

"You're going to have problems with us being teammates, aren't you?"

She sounded so wistful, he had to laugh. "It's going to take some work," he agreed.

Crossing to the door, he stopped and let his gaze linger on her freshly washed face and hair, her cute nose, her delicate chin. "Thanks for the toothbrush, razor and shirt. I can use all of it."

"You're welcome."

Living in the moment was unbearably tempting. The idea of sliding his body close to Gwen's and finding satisfaction with her was a primitive drumbeat pounding Garrett's good sense to smithereens. After he tore his gaze from hers, he stepped over the threshold into the bathroom and closed her door.

He regretted it as soon as he did it. It was one more regret on a list of too many to count.

Chapter Six

"Where do we go from here?" Gwen asked Garrett as they sat in his SUV in her driveway the next day after their return trip from Laramie.

She found she wasn't just asking about the case, but about them. During the trip Garrett had opened up to her, and she guessed that was rare for him. Last night she'd wanted very much to make love with him, yet she'd known neither of them was ready for that.

Now when his steady gray eyes acknowledged her deeper question, she held her breath.

"At least we know Amy's mother was likely from Laramie. It's luck that Flo struck up a conversation with the girl. Although we still don't know this young woman's name, we do have an accurate description—long straight brown hair, hazel eyes, about five-three."

"We also know her mother kicked her out when she got pregnant and she went to live with her boyfriend."

"I think it's time we put a composite sketch together. When I asked the sheriff if he had anyone who could do that, he said he didn't. Do you know any artists?"

"Lily Reynolds who owns Flutes and Drums has done some painting. Maybe she could do it."

"I'll find out."

Gwen hadn't slept last night. She had been too attuned to the fact that Garrett wasn't that far away. She'd been mulling over and reliving their kisses, their conversations, the magnetic pull between them. She'd never felt this interested, intrigued or turned on by a man before.

Unfastening his seat belt, Garrett shifted toward Gwen and laid his hand on her thigh. "What's the matter?"

"We're at a dead end. Even if you send that sketch to every police department in Wyoming, what are the chances someone will recognize this young woman?"

"You just never know. But we don't have to wait for that. I'm not finished in Wild Horse Junction yet."

His hand on her thigh sent heat radiating from the spot. "What do you mean?"

"Once I have a sketch in hand, once I talk to the convenience store clerk and the waitresses again—because both will have to give Lily Reynolds their input—we could unearth something else."

"We?" she asked with a teasing smile.

A twinkle danced in his eyes that she hadn't seen

there before. "Let's just say I've accepted the whole 'work as a team' thing."

The air in the SUV suddenly got thinner as her heart thudded. Before she thought better of it, she said honestly, "I enjoyed our trip to Laramie."

The twinkle was replaced by something darker. Primal hunger, maybe? Desire that went far beyond a few minutes of kissing? Although no rain fell, the day was still gray. Colder weather was moving in. In Garrett's SUV they were secluded from the world outside as well as the wind buffeting the vehicle. They were secluded from everyday concerns that didn't seem to have a place here.

"Maybe you're an adrenaline junkie and enjoy the thrill of chasing down a lead," Garrett offered, suppressing a smile.

"Maybe. Or maybe I just enjoyed your company," she admitted.

Quiet for a few moments, he finally responded, "What company is that? Most of our drive both ways was silent."

That was true. She thought about the long conversations she'd had with Mark…usually about their work. Yet she'd never felt as connected to Mark as she felt to Garrett. "Two people don't have to talk to enjoy being with each other."

"They sure as hell don't," he muttered leaning closer, lacing his fingers in her hair. With his other hand, he unfastened her seat belt.

Maybe Garrett believed they were safe now since they weren't near a bedroom, but she knew better. As soon as his lips crushed hers, as soon as his tongue slid into her mouth, as soon as his hand angled her head, she knew the two of them weren't safe no matter where they went. The chemistry between them was explosive. A word, a touch, a smile could land them in each other's arms.

She was flirting with the unknown, risking her heart, stirring up her life. Wasn't all of that reckless and so unlike her?

In Garrett's arms, she was a woman she didn't know—a woman who could dream again…a woman who could find satisfaction with a man…a woman who knew how to give pleasure and receive it.

After Garrett broke the kiss, he looked deep into her eyes, then kissed her all over again. This time his hands were as busy as his lips and tongue. They slid under her sweater, up her back and released her bra. Thoughts tumbled about in her head but she couldn't grab one. She could only feel.

Garrett's large callused hands on her back sent shivers through her and lit up sexual yearnings she'd never acknowledged. Mindlessly she reached for him, too. He'd worn the white T-shirt she'd bought him and now she frantically pulled it from his jeans. It was good to be in physical contact, to experience more of the toe-curling pleasure. Garrett might be a loner, but he was an experienced loner and knew how to kiss and how to touch.

He was a man who liked touching. She could tell just from the way he brought his hands around to her stomach, the way he gently dragged his fingers up her midriff to her breasts. When he cupped her, when he thumbed her nipples, tears came to her eyes from the sheer pleasure of it. The heat of his chest under his curling hair was scorching and she made a small circle with her hand, sliding over his tight abdominal muscles, letting her palm flatten to absorb as much about Garrett as she could from that simple touch.

Suddenly she felt the shift. She felt the change. She felt all of it ending. His hands dropped away from her and although his lips clung to hers for a few long moments, she knew he was going to pull away.

After he did, he leaned against his seat back and closed his eyes. His fingers wound about the steering wheel and then he gradually released it.

"This is broad daylight," he said gruffly.

"Would anything be different if we were in the dark?"

After he glanced at her, he smiled and shook his head. "You sure know the questions to ask, don't you? In the dark, I might not have stopped. In the dark, I might have convinced you to crawl into the backseat. In the dark—"

"You could forget who you were and who I was and just go with the flow?" She didn't want to think that, but maybe Garrett wasn't so different from other men she'd met.

Now he leaned forward and looked at her again. "I could *never* forget who you are."

Her breathing coming more evenly now, she responded, "I don't know if that's a compliment or not."

"I'm not sure, either," he grumbled.

She reached up under her sweater and refastened her bra, feeling a bit embarrassed now, maybe even a little used. Garrett had already told her he didn't want a relationship. He'd already told her he'd never marry again.

What was she doing? Deep down she knew that for her marriage had to be the final destination of a relationship.

The bag with the supplies she'd bought sat at her feet. She reached for it and the rustle of the plastic was loud in the car.

Garrett reached one long arm into the backseat and plucked up her jacket. When he handed it to her, his expression was unreadable. She wondered how long he'd had to practice not letting any emotion show—months…years? Had he begun practicing when his parents divorced?

"You'll let me know if you find anything else about Amy's mother?" she had to ask because a dead end might mean the end of the road, both for finding the baby's mother and for them.

"I'll let you know what happens with the sketch. I'll give Lily Reynolds a call when I get home."

Their time together *had* ended. The mission was finished for now. But she didn't want to get out of his SUV. And even though it went against everything she knew was right for her, she wanted to invite him inside.

She felt as shaken as she had the first day she'd laid eyes on Garrett Maxwell.

Opening her door, she climbed out. "I'll see you when I see you," she said flippantly. "Good luck with the sketch."

After she hurried up the walk to her front door and unlocked it, he backed out of her driveway and drove away.

Inside, the stillness and emptiness of the house caused a hollow feeling in her chest.

Maybe she needed to find a cat.

* * *

Garrett came home from his trip with Gwen a restless man. He never spilled his guts. He didn't confide in anyone. When he'd been married to Cheryl, she often accused him of being closemouthed, secretive, unwilling to share. He'd blamed his job and so had she.

The truth was, however, that he'd been self-sufficient and needed no one for as long as he could remember. His parents' bitter fights, the emotional darts they'd tossed at each other, the hurtful arrows they'd carefully aimed had taught him not to give personal information to anyone who could use it against him. Their divorce and then his chosen career had reinforced the fact. Ever since he'd returned to Wild Horse Junction, he'd kept his own counsel and liked it that way. Yet since he'd met Gwen, sometimes thoughts leaked out he never intended to voice. Her intuitive, yet probing questions nudged open doors he'd always thought were better kept closed.

Climbing the stairs to his loft, intending to add to the notes he'd inputted on the Baby Amy case, he opened the door to his office. It was an absolute mess. Several months of receipts lay scattered to the right of his computer monitor. Every day he expected to record them, but he hadn't found the time. Stacked file folders—about a foot of them—tilted precariously on a chair. The airplane mobile above them caught his eye and his gaze strayed and settled on the original 1983 *Return of the Jedi* poster on the wall. It didn't fit with the decor of the rest of the house any more than the mobile did, but he'd dragged it with him from his youth.

Trying to hold on to the kid he'd been? Trying to re-member more carefree days?

Focusing again on Baby Amy and the new informa-tion he'd learned, he switched on the computer, suddenly realizing he'd forgotten to check his mes-sages. He kept the machine in the kitchen since that was most convenient. He *never* forgot to check his mes-sages. But Gwen was on his mind...not someone who might want to hire him to ensure the security of their computer network.

A few minutes later, he stood at the kitchen counter and pushed the play button on the answering machine. The first message startled him. "Hey, Garrett. It's Cheryl. Give me a call when you can." She rattled off a number.

Cheryl? Now? Why? What could they possibly have to say to each other? They hadn't spoken in years!

Still wondering why she'd phoned, he listened to the second message. It was from Gwen's father. "Mr. Maxwell, it's Russ Langworthy. I stopped by your place, hoping to talk to you. Can you call me?" He gave Garrett his phone number then added, "I have an idea that could benefit us both."

Cheryl's voice still playing in his head, Garrett called the number his ex-wife had left. It was different from the one in his address book. Had she simply called to tell him she moved?

Cheryl never did anything "simply."

After her phone rang a few times, her voice mail clicked on. He didn't leave a message. If she had caller ID, she'd know he called. If she didn't...

They'd connect eventually.

Garrett dialed Russ Langworthy's number, not liking the tightness in his chest caused by thinking about Cheryl—too much history that brought up guilt and sadness.

Gwen's father picked up on the first ring.

"Mr. Langworthy, this is Garrett Maxwell. You tried to get hold of me?"

"Yes, I did. I went out to the hangar where you keep your plane. Nice Skyhawk you've got there."

Now what was Russ doing around his plane? "You got inside the hangar?" The doors were locked except when he or Dave Johnson, a mechanic he used, were working on the plane.

"Your mechanic was there. Friendly fellow. He was glad to give me a quick look before he left."

"Is there a reason you went to the hangar?"

"I was curious about your plane. As I told you at the barn dance, I flew in Nam."

Russ had generally spoken about manning a copter.

"When was the last time you flew?"

"Early seventies," Russ answered. "When I got home I wanted to forget about what happened over there. I got my CPA's license, met my wife, got married, and we adopted Gwen. After my wife left and I was drinking, I never considered flying again. Did Gwen tell you about any of that?"

"Some."

"Did she tell you I've been sober for three years now?"

"Congratulations."

"I didn't call you for a pat on the back. I called you

because…" He hesitated. "Because I thought maybe you could use some help."

"What kind of help?" Garrett asked warily.

"I got a hole in my life that needs filled, and I have experience you might find handy. I've also got twenty-twenty vision and on a search-and-rescue gig, that can be important. I'd like to volunteer to go with you."

Usually someone from the search team went up with Garrett to act as a spotter. However someone with spotting experience from the air wasn't always available. Distance perspective from the air was different than on the ground. Russ Langworthy had a trained eye for finding landing sights, signals, the enemy as well as the wounded. Still… "I don't know, Mr. Langworthy."

"It's Russ. I know this isn't something you want to make a snap decision on. In fact, my guess is, you want to say no. But before you do, just think about it. Think about an experienced pair of eyes with binoculars helping you search. Think about maybe spotting a kid a little faster."

Russ was right that Garrett wanted to say "no" but something held him back from doing that. "What makes you think this will fill up the hole in your life?"

"I don't know for sure. Maybe it won't. I still go to meetings. But I need to do something that doesn't have a payoff for me. You know what I mean?"

"There's a payoff. You'll be in the air again. You'll get an adrenaline rush from the search."

"Maybe so, but I've got to start somewhere and this just seems like a good place. Why do you do it?"

He did it because every time he found a child, he was making up for the one he'd lost. He was making up for his part in his marriage failing. He knew what *he* did wasn't altruistic because he was still assuaging his guilt.

"I do it for lots of reasons." He thought about Russ's suggestion again. "As you said, I can't make a snap decision on this. I never imagined having a partner."

"We could just try it once or twice. You could see how it goes. If it doesn't work out, I'll join a crew on Habitat for Humanity or something."

A smile crept onto Garrett's lips. "You know how to build houses?"

"Nope, but I can learn." After a pause he reminded Garrett, "I'll be waiting to hear from you and if the answer's no, don't worry about hurting my feelings. You just give it to me straight. And something else, Mr. Maxwell."

"It's Garrett."

"Okay, Garrett. This has nothing to do with Gwen."

"She doesn't know you're talking to me about this?"

"She doesn't know. I'd rather just keep it that way."

"If I decide to take you up with me even once, I wouldn't keep it from her. You shouldn't, either."

"Fair enough. I'll be waiting to hear from you."

When Garrett hung up the phone, he wasn't pleased to have yet another complication in his life. He'd been living a solitary existence that had suited him just fine.

Now he'd have to consider whether he wanted to change his life.

Or not.

On Tuesday, Gwen sat in her office recording the last of her patient notes when the receptionist buzzed her.

"Yes, Agnes," she answered absentmindedly, her attention on the notes on her desk.

"There's a man here to see you. Said his name is Garrett Maxwell."

Agnes suddenly had all of Gwen's attention. Garrett? Here? "Send him back, Agnes."

Mere seconds later, there was a rap on Gwen's door. She hurried to answer it and Garrett filled the doorway. She backed up so he could step inside.

As he did, he took up all the space in her cubbyhole of an office in his black windbreaker, black jeans and white T-shirt. Sometimes his sheer male presence took her breath away.

Most of the time.

"Has something happened?" She couldn't imagine why else he would be here.

"Yes, it has." He glanced down at something in his hand. It looked like a menu. "Mandy at The Silver Dollar called me. She was talking to another waitress on her break and the woman remembered our young couple. She also recalled the guy was doodling on the menu. The two of them searched through all of them and this is what she found."

He handed the menu to Gwen, back side up, and she studied it. It was a map of the area—of Wyoming's border into Montana. Someone had used a pen and drawn a circle around Little Creek.

"You think this is where they were headed?"

"It's a long shot, but it's a possibility. If flight conditions are suitable, I'm going to fly up. I can be there in an hour. I didn't know if you might want to come along."

Gwen glanced at the charts on her desk she was going to study for her next-day patients.

"I had two patients cancel this afternoon, so I'm free relatively speaking. If we leave now, it'll be dark when we fly back."

Garrett's eyes twinkled with some amusement. "Planes fly in the dark."

"I know, but isn't it more dangerous in a small plane?"

"I have my instrument rating, Gwen. My plane's in A-1 condition and I know what I'm doing. If you don't want to go, that's fine. I'll nose around on my own."

"I want to go."

"But?"

"I've never been up in a small plane before."

"There's a first time for everything," he commented sardonically, and her head was suddenly filled with visions other than of plane rides.

A first time making love with Garrett.

Would he be intense and focused as a lover? Could he be playful? Would he let his guard down? Would the hunger for each other take over and nothing else matter?

Gwen told herself not to go there. She was considering a plane ride, not tangling the sheets with Garrett. But the two experiences seemed to have exciting somersault-sensation similarities.

She made an impulsive decision before her courage deserted her. "Let me get the medical bag I use for home visits and I'll be ready." One look at Garrett and she knew what he was going to say.

"I know we might not find her. I know this could be a disappointing ride. But I like to be prepared."

After a long steady look, he said, "I'll meet you at the airport."

An hour and a half later, it was almost dark when they touched down on the landing field in Little Creek, Montana. Gwen had been nervous before they'd taken off, but she'd soon realized Garrett was an experienced pilot and knew exactly what he was doing. His conversation with the mechanic at the hangar, his methodical preflight check had eased her into the idea of flying with him. In the air the views had been magnificent, and although they could communicate with headsets, they'd flown most of the trip in silence.

As soon as the plane was secured, a Blazer came barreling out to it. When Garrett opened the passenger door, the man in the driver's seat, who had to be at least seventy and out in the sun most of his life, grinned widely. "Hey, Garrett. It's been a while."

"A couple of years. Thanks for meeting us."

"No problem. I owe you." To Gwen he explained, "Garrett came up here to look for my grandson, even though he'd just run after a jackrabbit to our ranch's north fork."

Garrett made quick introductions and Gwen liked Ed Randolph right away. She learned he owned a ranch a few miles out of town and Garrett had called him before he'd left Wild Horse.

As Garrett let her ride in the front seat beside Ed, she followed the conversation of the two men catching up.

Five minutes later, Ed parked in front of a run-down motel. "You think the girl you're looking for is here?" he asked Garrett as he wrinkled his nose at the place.

"I called around this afternoon. The motel owner said a guy rented the room a week ago. He had his girlfriend with him but she didn't go in or out. Three days ago he left a hundred and fifty dollars with the clerk. The owner suspects she doesn't have any more money and tomorrow's her last day. Since she doesn't have a car, and her boyfriend didn't say he'd be back, he's glad someone's inquiring about her. She's in room three."

Garrett had given Gwen this information soon after they'd taken off.

"I'll wait here," Ed told them as they climbed out.

At the door to number three, Garrett took hold of Gwen's elbow and she could feel the imprint of his hand all the way down to her toes.

"This could be anyone," he warned her.

In that instant, she saw that Garrett didn't want her to get hurt, didn't want her to be disappointed. Like a thunderbolt, she also realized she was falling hard for this man, even though she knew she shouldn't. Falling, not just because of the attraction, but because of who he was.

Taking a deep breath, postponing examining her feelings further, she whispered, "Whoever she is, it sounds as if she might need someone's help."

"You'd adopt the whole world if you could, wouldn't you?" he asked seriously.

"Yes, I would. Wouldn't you?"

Garrett didn't answer her, just released her arm and knocked on the door.

Gwen's heart thudded. What were the chances that whoever was in this motel room was Amy's mother? She thought of the baby, rocking her, cooing to her, snuggling her tight. If Amy's mother was here, then what?

One step at a time, she warned herself as she cast a glance at Garrett.

As was usually the case, his face was expressionless. His body, however, held restrained energy she blamed on expectation.

He knocked again, louder.

When still no one came, he called, "Is anyone in there? If so, please open up. If you don't, the manager will unlock the door for us."

His voice was authoritarian…official-sounding. If she were inside, would she open up or want to run?

Gwen heard shuffling close to the door, the lock being turned, then someone pulled open the door a crack, only as far as the chain bolt would allow.

Gwen was surprised a motel that was run-down like this even *had* chain bolts!

A weak female voice asked, "Who are you?"

Garrett answered calmly, "We're looking for Amy's mother."

When Gwen heard a gasp, and then a small sob, she nudged Garrett and he let her stand in the space he'd occupied. "Please open the door so we can talk to you. We want to help. I'm the one who found Amy. Are you her mom?"

The sound of the young woman crying was wrenching, and Gwen knew Garrett just wanted to break off that chain bolt. She felt the same way. But they both waited.

Gwen repeated softly, "We want to help you, really we do. Amy's doing well. She was placed with a foster family. But if you're her mom, do you really want her there? Don't you want her with you?"

Fumbling fingers unfastened the chain. Finally the door opened and they were staring at a young woman with tears coursing down her cheeks. Her straight brown hair was disheveled. She was starkly pale and her hazel eyes looked much too big for her face.

Wearing baggy jeans with holes in them and an oversize T-shirt, she choked back a sob and put her fist to her mouth. "I can't keep her. I don't have any money and Justin left me here. I don't think he cares about us at all."

Unable to help herself, Gwen stepped forward and wrapped her arm around the girl's shoulders. The teenager was trembling, and Gwen didn't like the pasty color of her face. This young woman had been through hell—definitely emotionally and probably physically, too—from the looks of her.

"Let's go over here and sit down." She gently guided the girl to the bed. Over her shoulder to Garrett, she directed, "Get my bag, will you?"

A look crossed his face that said he wasn't used to taking orders, especially not from a woman. He also, obviously, didn't want to let her alone with the girl. But he turned and strode to the SUV.

"What's your name?" she asked as the teenager sank onto the bed as if she had no energy to hold her up.

"It's Tiffany."

Still keeping her arm around the girl, Gwen tried to put her at ease. "I'm Gwen. And I'm a nurse."

"I know who you are," Tiffany whispered.

Tiffany's face looked familiar, but where Gwen had had contact with the girl wasn't important now. "Will you let me check you over?"

Instead of answering, the girl asked a question of her own. "Are they going to put me in jail?"

"I don't know what's going to happen," Gwen responded truthfully. "We'll have to sort it all out. Do you want to give up Amy?"

"No! But I don't have any choice. My mother threw me out. She wanted me to have an abortion. So did Justin. When I told him I wouldn't, that I had no place to go, he wasn't sure what to do with me, but he let me stay with him. I…" Her voice faded and she suddenly went even paler.

"Lay back," Gwen suggested, helping her stretch out on the bed, taking the pillow and propping it under her knees. She lifted Tiffany's wrist to check her pulse. When she glanced at the girl's drawn face, Gwen saw her eyes were closed. "Stay with me, here."

When there was no answer, Gwen prodded again. "Come on, Tiffany. Open your eyes and look at me." The teenager's pulse was fast and Gwen calculated it while she checked her watch.

With a rush of male presence, Garrett returned to the room and handed Gwen her bag. "Is she sick?"

"My guess is she's dehydrated and malnourished to begin with. I'm not sure what else is going on. How close is the nearest hospital?"

"Billings."

After another look at the girl, he added, "I can have her back in Wild Horse Junction almost as fast as we can get to Billings. I can call ahead and have an ambulance meet us at the airport."

Gwen didn't like Tiffany's color or the clamminess of her skin. "Let me examine her. And see if you can find something to eat that isn't all sugar. Water to drink, too."

She noticed the candy wrappers scattered on the nightstand, the empty cans of soda sitting on the floor.

Opening her bag, Gwen took out her stethoscope. She was putting it to her ears when Garrett left the room.

Chapter Seven

Gwen paced the waiting area down the hall from Tiffany's room at St. Luke's Hospital in Wild Horse Junction. When Garrett came in, she stopped pacing.

As he came to her, a concerned expression was etched on his face. "I saw a doctor is in with Tiffany. Are you all right?"

She wasn't. She was worried about Tiffany and Amy and the whole situation. However, she assured him, "I'm fine."

An ambulance had met them at the airport, and Tiffany had insisted Gwen ride with her. Garrett had had to take care of his plane and lock up the hangar for the night.

"Did you have to wait long in the emergency room?" he asked.

"Just long enough for a doctor to look her over and me to fill out papers. When they decided to admit her, I requested Dr. Phillips." Marsha Phillips was her own gynecologist and one of the doctors in the practice she worked for.

"Are you covering her expenses?" Garrett asked, his brows raised.

"For now. Until we get some official forms filled out. I called Shaye. Family Services has to be aware we found her. And I also called Walter Ludlow."

"The lawyer?"

"Yes. Shaye's worked with him and so has Dylan. In fact he and Dylan are good friends. Tiffany's going to need an advocate. Even if Shaye goes to bat for her, that might not be enough."

"You're getting too involved," Garrett warned her.

"*Too* involved? Just what is that, Garrett? You heard Tiffany's story as well as I did." Gwen had kept Tiffany talking in the SUV on the way to the plane, not wanting her to pass out.

"You've got to be realistic about this, Gwen."

"I *am* being realistic. She has no one, certainly not the mother who threw her out when she was pregnant. Even if we found her boyfriend, what kind of kid is he to take her to the apartment of some guy he doesn't even know that well after she delivers and needs medical care? And when they get tossed out of there, dump her in some motel with no money and no way home?" Gwen was exasperated and felt as if she wanted to shake some sense into someone, mostly Tiffany's mother who hadn't acted as a parent should—supportive and loving.

Crossing his arms over his chest, Garrett shook his head. "Only a boy with no sense," he agreed.

Gwen could only imagine how difficult the whole ordeal must have been for Tiffany…how scared she'd been. "As weak as she was, she didn't have the energy to fight him. She wants to be a mother to her baby. She just didn't see any way she could be."

"She abandoned her child."

"She did *not* abandon her," Gwen protested hotly. "She left her with me. There's a big difference."

While Garrett had carried Tiffany to the plane, Gwen had finally remembered where she'd seen her. Last March, Gwen had gone to Laramie and given a workshop to high school teachers about unwed mothers and how the staff could prepare them for motherhood. She'd also given a presentation for any junior and senior girls who'd wanted to attend—they could ask questions about anything. In the workshop, Gwen had shared realities about raising a child in the twenty-first century, about how important health care could be to these young women. Tiffany hadn't asked any questions, but she'd been in that audience. Apparently she'd also read the write-up about Gwen that had appeared in the Laramie paper.

After Tiffany had her baby in her boyfriend's apartment, there'd been so much blood she'd been weak afterward. He told her they couldn't care for Amy. *He* couldn't care for Amy and they had to do something. Tiffany had remembered Gwen. She'd told Justin there was somebody in Wild Horse Junction who would take Amy and know what was best for her. That day he had seen Gwen in her backyard after work. After she'd gone inside, he'd found the sliding door was unlocked and had set the baby in the sunroom. Apparently he'd watched to make sure Gwen found Amy, then high-tailed it out of there. After getting something to eat and a few supplies in Wild Horse, they'd driven north and stayed with a friend of Justin's. When he kicked them out they'd checked in at the motel. Tiffany was still weak and sick from the delivery, and Justin didn't know what to do with her. When she'd awakened on the fourth morning, he'd left without her, leaving a note saying he couldn't take her with him because he couldn't afford her medical care and she'd slow him down.

"You called Shaye and I can understand that," Garrett said with a frown. "But the lawyer? Who's going to pay his fee? How's that girl going to take care of a baby when she can't take care of herself?"

"Men!" Gwen lifted her hands in exasperation. "All you think about is money, black-and-white and a straight road without any curves in it. If you don't want to be involved in this, that's fine, then walk away. Your job's done. But maybe I can do more. Maybe I can help Tiffany keep her baby. Maybe I can even give them a place to stay."

That blew the neutral expression from Garrett's face. "You're not serious."

"I'm very serious."

"Do you have *any* idea of the responsibility you'd be taking on?"

She almost laughed at the irony of the question. "I understand responsibility, Garrett. After all, I took care of myself and a grown man for years."

Garrett dragged his fingers through his hair. "This is different."

"Yes, it is. I think I'm a good judge of character and I believe Tiffany just needs a chance. She's a smart girl. Before the doctor came in to examine her, she told me about the extra courses she's taken in summer school. Not because she had to, but because she wanted to. She has computer skills and secretarial skills, and she just needs a little help and a second chance." For some suddenly illogical reason, tears came to Gwen's eyes and she turned away from Garrett, blinking and willing the emotion to subside.

One of his large hands capped her shoulder. The other one took her elbow and nudged her around.

She couldn't look at him. She just couldn't. Looking into Garrett's eyes made her want to cry even more and she *wasn't* a crying woman.

His voice was soft and tender as he murmured, "Gwen," and took her into his arms.

"I'm fine," she mumbled against his chest.

"I know you are." His jaw rested on top of her head.

"I'm just worried about Tiffany's health and whether the sheriff is going to arrest her or not. I wish Walter would get here."

"And on top of all that, it's the end of the search. We found her."

Was that part of the problem, too? Garrett's part in this was over and Gwen knew he was going to walk away? He didn't want to be involved with her and why should he stay involved with Tiffany?

She didn't want him to walk away. She wasn't just

falling for Garrett Maxwell, she'd *fallen*. Too soon, too fast, too hard.

Pulling away from him, she looked up and was afraid too much of her emotions shone in her eyes.

"Gwen," he said again. There was pain and reluctance and regret in his voice.

Thank goodness he didn't have a chance to tell her he was going back to his own life.

Two men walked into the waiting room. One was Sheriff Thompson and the other was Walter Ludlow.

Garrett leaned close to her ear. "I'll take the sheriff, while you fill in Ludlow. We'll make this happen if you think Tiffany deserves it, but I hope you know what you're doing because your life is never going to be the same."

At that moment, Gwen saw her life changing as a good thing.

Stepping away from Garrett, she extended her hand to Walter Ludlow and smiled.

Garrett sat in Gwen's driveway waiting for her to finish with her home health-care visits. He found himself impatient for her to return home and was unsure why. Because of the idea he had? He had to be damn sure it was something he wanted to do.

As she drove down the street, she saw him and waved. A few minutes later, he was standing in her living room, telling her, "I flew to Laramie and met with Tiffany's mother. Mrs. Morrison is *not* the motherly type."

Gwen looked surprised. He'd surprised himself by confronting the woman.

"What did she say?" Gwen asked, her cheeks reddening.

"She said Tiffany's eighteen and on her own. She's not taking care of some bastard kid and Tiffany better not ask her for anything because she doesn't have anything to give her."

"I can't believe any mother would act that way… would be so hardhearted that she'd turn her daughter away."

"Believe me, it wasn't an act. She doesn't have much, Gwen, and what she does have, she wants to keep, not share with Tiffany. I got the impression Tiffany's a responsibility she didn't want to begin with, and she's been marking time until Tiffany turned eighteen and she could legally wash her hands of her."

"Tiffany told me she never knew her father," Gwen said softly, and Garrett realized she was already attached to the teenager.

She went to the phone. "I'm going to call Walter."

Crossing to her, Garrett stayed her hand. The electric thrill of touching her again was immediate and potent, but he withstood it. "Are you really going to take in Tiffany and the baby if the judge will let you?"

"Yes. It's the only chance Tiffany has of keeping Amy."

"And you're prepared for the fact that this could be temporary or permanent, that she could leave at any time, or she could stay forever?"

"She won't stay forever," Gwen responded almost sadly. "Tiffany wants to be on her own, taking care of Amy. Right now she doesn't have the means and doesn't know how."

"And when she does have the means…if she learns

to care for Amy, are you going to be able to back off and let her *be* the mother?"

"Why so many questions, Garrett? I thought you wanted to be done with this."

He saw in her eyes that she thought he wanted to be done with *her.* He'd given that a lot of thought. He'd been awake most of last night, telling himself he was the wrong man for Gwen. Yet there was something that drew him back to her over and over.

Maybe his life could use a change, too.

"I spoke with Tiffany this morning before I left for Laramie."

Gwen's astonishment showed. "What about?"

"I wanted to see if your assessment of her was correct. I wanted to find out exactly what she could do in the real world—as in getting a job. They're not that easy to find in Wild Horse right now."

"I'm sure there's some business that needs a secretary…some business that could use an office worker."

"There is. Me."

Stunned, Gwen's mouth opened. She closed it and asked incredulously, "You?"

Just as he'd lined up the practical reasons in his head, he listed them now. "Security businesses generate paperwork. Some days I can't get any work done because of the calls I have to take and make. Last night when I got home, there were seven that had to be answered. I had no time to return them today. Not to mention the fact my files should be reorganized, my backup information needs to be labeled and stored and I have a stack of book work that has to be entered into the computer.

Tiffany will look more adult and capable to the judge if she has a job going into the hearing, don't you think? With me she could ease into work and even bring the baby with her."

"You'd want a baby in your house?"

Her question let loose pain he'd held inside ever since Cheryl had lost their baby. "It will be okay. Besides, you'll be on call if we need you."

Gwen was wearing a herringbone blazer, silk blouse and camel slacks. Even at the end of the day, she smelled flowery and fruity and all he wanted to do was gather her into his arms.

As she stepped closer to him, her eyes were full of questions. "Why are you doing this, Garrett? I'm looking forward to taking care of Tiffany and her baby. I'm looking forward to having them be part of my life and part of my family. Are you just giving a needy teenager a leg up? Do you think this is going to be easy? Because it's not. Babies cry. Tiffany will get frustrated—"

"I lost the chance to have a baby around my house. Maybe I just want to see what it's like. I'm not committing myself to being her father or even a big brother. I'll be her employer."

Gwen moved even closer, raised her hand, and tapped the left side of his chest with her palm. "I think you put on a good act. I think you pretend to be a tough guy one hundred percent of the time, but there's a big heart in you with lots of tender spots."

When he covered her hand with his, he shook his head. "I'm just trying to make up for past sins."

"That's what you believe, but I think you want more than you're going to let yourself have."

He'd stopped wanting when he'd stopped dreaming, but now the wants toppled over each other and all of them seemed to have something to do with Gwen.

Still trying to keep her at a distance, he responded gruffly, "You think you know me. You don't."

"In some ways, I think I know you better than you know yourself."

"If you truly knew me, you'd be running in the other direction."

"Because…"

"Because I want to do things with you I've never wanted to do with any other woman."

If she had said something, maybe he would have backed away. If she had issued an invitation, he probably could have turned it down. But all she did was stand there, looking at him with those velvet-brown eyes, her pink lips parted, her multitude of curls framing her face. She didn't try to cover her freckles with makeup and he found that fact altogether sexy. He found *everything* about her sexy.

With a deep groan, he kissed the freckles, then her cheeks, then her open lips. He hadn't taken off his jacket. He'd intended this visit to be short and sweet. Now he shrugged it off and opened her blazer, pushed it back, and off her shoulders. Her breasts thrust forward and her silk blouse didn't hide much. He didn't need X-ray vision to see the lacy bra. He didn't need a sixth sense to know her panties probably matched.

Lace and silk and Gwen.

As he tried to unbutton her blouse, she pulled his T-shirt from his jeans. Her bra was as flimsy as a butterfly's wings. With the top half of her naked, he finally took her into his arms and kissed her…kissed her hard.

Somehow they landed on the sofa. He broke away from her long enough for her to pull his T-shirt over his head. They were a tangle of arms as his mouth pressed hers again and their tongues mated. He thought about breathing and decided it wasn't necessary. Only kissing Gwen was necessary. Only touching her soft satiny skin was necessary. Her desire seemed to rival his and that was new for him—that both of them wanted sex as much as he did.

She apparently could do two things at once. She was responding to his kiss and searching for his belt buckle at the same time. He should get her out of her slacks, somehow push off his boots and drop his jeans. But right now all he could think about were her fingers near his fly. The belt buckle wouldn't give and apparently fed up with it, she reached underneath and unfastened his zipper. He knew she could feel him straining to be free. He knew she was probably wet and ready.

How could this hunger have overtaken them so fast? Were they still primed from spending the night in the B-and-B together? They'd wanted each other that night, too, but they'd had enough sense not to tangle their lives and emotions any more than they already were.

What had happened tonight?

Impulse, overstimulation, acquiescence. Surrender was easier than the battle they were fighting. Denial was growing old. Bonds between them were growing.

Bonds.

Gwen was going to establish bonds with Tiffany and Amy. She was the most compassionate, giving woman he'd ever met. But he couldn't see himself in her picture. He'd proved he wasn't a family man. To be one, he'd have to give up everything he thought was important to him. Gwen's biological parents abandoned her. Her adoptive mother abandoned her.

He was the wrong man for her.

How would she cope with him searching for kids at the drop of a hat, at the ring of a pager, at the beep of a cell phone? Would she feel he was leaving her over and over again? He'd made promises to Cheryl but those promises had had different meanings for both of them. He didn't make promises anymore. If he didn't make them, he wouldn't break them. Gwen Langworthy was the type of woman who needed a man with a nine-to-five, down-to-earth job who would put her first.

Gwen's fingers slipped into his fly. When he sucked in a breath, she caressed him.

Nobility was going to kill him.

He broke the kiss and tried to get his breathing under control.

"What?" she asked, her cheeks flushed, her eyes bright, her voice husky with the passion he was feeling, too. "Do you want to take off your jeans?" she asked.

Gwen didn't beat around the bush. She was straightforward and honest and he had to be, too, even if it hurt her.

Dragging in a long draft of air, he laid his hand over hers and stopped her fingers from making him even crazier. "I can't do this."

She looked perplexed. "You don't have a condom?"

Oh, he had a condom—just in case a situation like this came up with her, just in case he'd wanted to take advantage of mindless, hungry desire. "That's not the problem. *We're* the problem."

Her fingers went still under his, her expression changed…became guarded…became wary. "I don't want to hear this, do I?"

"You know what I'm going to say, Gwen. We've been over this before."

"Then why does this keep happening? Why can't we stay away from each other? You didn't have to go see Tiffany's mother. You didn't have to come here and tell me what she said. You could have just called. You could have passed on the message through Shaye or Walter."

"We've been working together on this."

"Yes, we have." Looking away from him, she spotted her blouse near the sofa. Disconnecting her hand from his, she reached for it and hurriedly put it on. As she fastened the buttons, her gaze met his again. "You offered to give Tiffany a job. Did you mean it?"

"Yes, I meant it. But my giving her a job doesn't have to have anything to do with us."

After a long look into his eyes, she blew out a breath. "No, I guess it doesn't. I guess you know how to compartmentalize everything. Fine. I'll just have to learn how to do that, too. I'll help Tiffany look for another job. If she can't find anything else, she'll have to take yours. There aren't many employers who will let her bring a baby."

"That's if she keeps custody. There's no saying that's going to happen."

"If you and I go to bat for her, as well as Shaye and Walter, she has a chance."

Garrett clasped Gwen's arm. "If we have sex, we'll both be sorry afterward."

"There you go, drawing conclusions for me again." She shook her head and stood. "You need to go to training camp for ex-FBI agents. Maybe there they can teach you how to drop the macho attitude."

"I don't have—"

"Yes, you do." She looked down the hall to her bedroom. "I'm going to put myself together and then go over to Shaye's. She and I are going to sort through some baby things Timmy's outgrown. You can get dressed and let yourself out."

Standing, she moved away from the sofa and with one smooth motion, snatched up her bra. Then she disappeared down the hall.

If he went after her…

They'd solve nothing.

Maybe he didn't need a solution. He needed a way to sever the bonds that had formed with Gwen. For both their sakes.

Chapter Eight

Where was Tiffany?

When Gwen came home from work on Monday, she expected to find Tiffany in her room or on the couch...or sitting in the sunroom. But she wasn't any of those places and there was no note.

Going to the phone, Gwen wasn't sure who to call. When she'd brought Tiffany home from the hospital on Thursday, the teenager had still been weak and tired. But by yesterday, she'd been looking much better. Gwen guessed her remaining lethargy was as much emotional as it was physical.

Had she run again? Had the whole situation over-whelmed her?

Then suddenly Gwen knew. She had spoken to Tiffany

about her hearing tomorrow. Gwen knew they had to be realistic, but with Garrett's job waiting and a place to stay until Tiffany could truly become independent, Gwen was hoping for the best and had told Tiffany that.

Still, she remembered the eighteen-year-old asking, "But what if the judge takes my baby away from me forever?"

Gwen was about to call Amy's foster parents when the front door opened. Tiffany came in looking tired but otherwise in one piece. Last week Gwen had bought her jeans and a couple of sweaters to tide her over until they could go shopping together. She was wearing her own jacket now, a yellow windbreaker trimmed in purple.

Realizing this was her first stab at being a surrogate parent, Gwen wanted to do it right. "I was worried," she said simply.

Tiffany sank down into the armchair. Her excursion, no matter where she'd gone, had tired her out. "Sorry. I thought about leaving a note, but I didn't want you to be upset."

"Why would I have been upset?"

Unzipping her jacket, Tiffany shrugged out of it and pushed her long hair over her shoulder. "I went to see Amy." She rushed on as if Gwen was going to interrupt. "I had to see her, can't you understand that? After tomorrow, I might never see her again. What if the judge puts me in jail? What if he gives her to a strange family who doesn't care about her? I had to see where she was and how she was."

There was accusation in Tiffany's eyes. "I meant for her to stay with *you*."

"In pioneer days it might have been that simple," Gwen explained calmly. "If you wanted someone else to take care of your baby, you gave her to them. But now it's not like that. There's paperwork and a judicial process."

"I knew you would take good care of her."

Gwen wasn't going to mention the fact that Tiffany had only heard her speak, heard her talk to a few students and read her credentials. "I know that, and I'm honored. But your case is going to the judge because everyone wants to look out for Amy's best interests."

"I'm so scared," Tiffany whispered, looking down at her hands. She folded them together and didn't look up.

After she crossed to her, Gwen crouched down, taking Tiffany's hands in hers. "I know you are. But I think the caseworker's visit on Friday went well." A social worker had made a home visit to interview Tiffany as well as to examine the living conditions Gwen could provide. "The sheriff didn't file charges against you after Mr. Ludlow talked to him," Gwen added reassuringly. "And Walter is very experienced."

Walter Ludlow was almost seventy and he had a good reputation among his peers and with the members of the judiciary.

"I'm hoping the judge will listen to him and take his recommendation," Gwen added.

"Are you sure Mr. Maxwell will be there?" Tiffany asked with worry in her hazel eyes. "He hasn't been around."

No, Garrett hadn't been around. Because of the way they'd parted? Because she cared too much and he was afraid to care?

"Mr. Ludlow told me he notified Mr. Maxwell of the time he's supposed to be there tomorrow. He said he'll be there."

"People don't always do what they say they're going to do," Tiffany mumbled.

"The people you've known before haven't, but these people do."

When Gwen's phone rang, she patted Tiffany's arm and went to get it.

Shaye was on the other end of the line. "Were the Renards upset?" Gwen asked, knowing why Shaye was calling. The foster family most probably had called her.

"They were more surprised than upset," Shaye replied. "Tiffany showed up on their doorstep looking like a lost waif. They called me right away just to let me know what was happening."

"And?"

"And they could easily see she just wanted to be with her baby. She's a bright girl. She told them she knew she didn't have any right to be there but she didn't know what was going to happen with the judge and she couldn't bear not to touch little Amy's face again. They let her hold her and rock her and feed her."

Gwen asked the question that had concerned her most. "Did she get in trouble by going there?"

"No. Nothing's been decided yet. After all, she's still Amy's mother. If anything, the judge might look on her visit kindly. I just don't know."

"This is all new to me," Gwen admitted, looking over at Tiffany.

"I get that. Just remember, when I brought Timmy

home, I hadn't dreamed about being a mother over-night, either. You're going to do great."

Gwen lowered her voice. "But she's eighteen. I'm not so sure she *needs* a mother."

"I'm twenty-nine. I still miss my mother and wish she were here. That doesn't change." Shaye had been ten when her mother died. Gwen had been six when her adoptive mother left. She knew Shaye was right.

"Will the foster parents be at the hearing tomorrow?"

"They won't have a part in the hearing since this is about Tiffany and whether or not she should have custody of her baby. But I've heard the judge wants them there because he wants to see Amy. My guess is, he intends to examine how Tiffany acts around her. He'll probably ask her to hold her."

"She's never been around babies before."

"From what I understand, Gwen, she did a good job today. No matter what, she has to be natural and tell the truth. This judge will see through anything else. I understand Tiffany's mother won't be coming to the hearing."

Walter had notified the woman, requesting her pres-ence, but she'd refused to come. "Tiffany's mother could care less about the hearing. From what Garrett tells me, she doesn't know anything about the word 'support.' Tiffany earned all her good grades on her own, studying with friends, staying away from home a lot. She thought she wasn't wanted there, especially when her mother brought in new guys. So she made herself scarce and her mother liked it that way."

"Your heart's breaking for her, isn't it?"

To Shaye, she could easily confide, "Yes, it is. I see so much of me in her."

"What does Garrett think about you taking this on?"

"I don't know what he thinks, and it really doesn't matter."

"Oh, I think it matters. You just won't admit it. Are you doing this to make the relationship with Garrett even more difficult?"

"Don't be ridiculous! The one has nothing to do with the other. They just sort of happened simultaneously. If Garrett and I see each other or if we don't, that's separate from the family I want to build with Tiffany and Amy."

"You don't want him to be part of that family?" her friend asked knowingly.

"I'd love it if he would be. I'd love it if he could wholeheartedly be a role model for Tiffany and Amy. But he had years of training and work that have kept him guarded. Once in a while, he gives me a piece of who he truly is, but afterward I think he regrets it."

"You both need time to absorb everything that's happening. He might need time to let his guard down with you, but you need time to learn to trust again."

"That's just it, Shaye, I think Garrett is a man I can trust. He inspires confidence. When he wants to be, he can be protective and caring." She took a deep breath. "I can't be wrong twice, can I?"

"That depends on how deep you're looking, and exactly how much you dig into his life and he digs into yours. Was he married before?"

"Yes, he was."

"Poke around. See how he reacts. Find out how he left it. Past marriages can give you a wealth of information."

"Garrett won't let me poke very deeply. That's a problem. Right now, I can only concentrate on Tiffany's hearing. I just want it to go her way. I want to help her to be a mother to Amy and then let her take over on her own."

"You'll have to decide if you want to be *Aunt* Gwen or *Grandma* Gwen."

She laughed. "Now *that's* a decision to make."

"Don't go buying granny glasses yet," Shaye teased.

There were a few beats of silence, then Gwen said, "Thank you for watching over Amy like this."

"It's my job. That's why I sent someone impartial to do that home visit on Friday."

"Can you tell me about the report?"

"That was sealed for the judge. He'll let you know what's in it. Relax tonight, Gwen, and try to get Tiffany to do the same. It could be the last night you both get a good night's sleep."

"Wouldn't that be wonderful?" Gwen asked seriously.

"Only a potential mother-to-be or someone who wants kids very much would say that. By the way, Dylan packed the SUV with all the baby things you picked out. If the hearing goes Tiffany's way, all you have to do is call him and he'll bring them over. The only essential thing you'll have to purchase is a crib."

"And I can do that in fifteen minutes if I have to. Do you really think I'm going to sleep tonight with everything buzzing in my head?"

Shaye laughed sympathetically. "You could always learn to knit. I hear that's trendy right now."

Gwen thought about the little sweater Bonnie had made to keep some child warm. "Maybe I will take up knitting. After all, I'm going to be the first-line babysitter."

"When Kylie's baby is born, we'll have a trio."

Holding no illusions, Gwen knew once Tiffany stood on her own two feet, she'd be moving out. Deep in her heart, Gwen wanted her own child, even if she didn't have a husband to go along with it. When she thought about the word *husband,* Garrett Maxwell's face popped up before her eyes. However, he'd been clear that a picket fence didn't fit into his life.

"To give you something else to think about, I sent out the invitations for Kylie's baby shower. Are you still planning to make a taco casserole?"

"Yes. I'll bring veggies and dip, too. It's coming up fast." They'd planned the shower for the second Sunday in November…only a month away.

"Try to get some sleep tonight," Shaye advised.

"I will."

After Gwen hung up, she went to Tiffany and smiled. "How about grilled turkey and cheese sandwiches with tomato soup? We can make a fresh salad, too, to go with it."

"You don't have to cook for me," Tiffany was quick to assure her, as if she didn't want to be a bother. "I can get my own."

"Some nights I might work late and you'll have to get your own. For tonight, I think it will be nice to eat together, don't you?"

After swallowing hard, Tiffany's gaze met Gwen's. Tears were bright in her eyes. "I'd like that a lot."

Already Gwen felt close to this girl. And that was almost as scary as loving Garrett.

Loving Garrett.

She'd tumbled over the edge, she suddenly realized. Now where did she go from here?

It was over.

Garrett thought about the hearing he'd just attended…the happiness in everybody's faces as the judge had warned Tiffany he'd be keeping a watchful eye on her and so would family services. For six months there would be sporadic home visits, and Tiffany had to report to a court-appointed counselor once a month. At the end of the six months, he'd evaluate her case again and make a final ruling.

The glow on Tiffany's face as well as Gwen's made Garrett feel as if he'd been a part of something huge today…like when he'd rescued a child. In this case, the feelings were much more personal, and that's what bothered him most. He hadn't spoken to Gwen. She and Tiffany had arrived at the meeting later than he had, right before the judge came in. Afterward, they'd been concerned with Amy and only Amy…as it should be.

But now…

He and Gwen had solved the case, and he felt like celebrating. He really should get to know Tiffany a little better before she started working under his roof.

So—

He drove to the discount store and asked the way to the infant section. When he stopped in front of something called a play saucer, he crouched down to examine it more closely. A cart rounded the corner of the aisle, and he was surprised to see Gwen and Tiffany.

Tiffany had Amy settled against her chest in one of those cloth baby carriers, while Gwen pushed the cart with a huge box almost toppling off of it. She was trying to push with one hand and hold the box with the other.

He heard her say, "The clerk said it's the last one. We're lucky. Now all we have to do is figure out how to put it together."

When he rose to his feet, Gwen stopped suddenly.

"Imagine seeing you here," he said as casually as he could.

"I think seeing *you* here is the bigger surprise," she blurted out.

"I thought I'd celebrate the good results of this case by getting Amy something."

"Oh, you don't have to do that, Mr. Maxwell," Tiffany assured him. "You've done enough. Without you, without your job, I don't know if the judge would have given me Amy," she finished shyly with all sincerity.

"I think you and Gwen would have come up with another job. I thought the saucer might come in handy as Amy gets bigger. It might keep her occupied while you're working. I hear babies grow fast."

As Tiffany giggled, she looked down at her daughter. "I don't know what to expect. I guess I'd better read up on it. Mrs. Malloy gave me a few books she used with Timmy."

Gwen had been watching their interchange, and now

he motioned to the huge box positioned on her cart. "Are you going to need some help with that?"

"You mean carrying it or putting it together?" she asked with a straight face.

"Either...both. I worked long into the night last night getting a project finished, so today I'm clearing my head."

"It's up to you, Garrett. If you want to help, that's fine with us."

She was acting as if she didn't care if he helped or not. He *wanted* her to care. "I'll follow you home. It might take more than one pair of hands to put together the crib *and* the saucer."

Tiffany had walked down the aisle a bit but was talking animatedly to her little daughter, pointing out the things she'd need as she grew older.

"You don't have better things to do this afternoon?" Gwen asked him, all kinds of questions in her eyes he didn't have the answers to.

"I probably do, but Tiffany seemed a little awkward around me. I thought it might be a good idea to try to establish a rapport with her before we start working together."

As if that answered many of Gwen's questions, her eyes lost their sparkle as she nodded, "That makes sense."

It made lots of sense....

Until Garrett was in Gwen's house again, inhaling her scent, letting her assist him and separating the crib's parts. Amy was crying and Gwen kept glancing over her shoulder into the living room with a worried expression on her face.

"It's hard to know when to help out and when *not* to

help, isn't it?" Garrett asked as he attached the side of the crib to the end.

"Yes, it is. She told me she wants to take care of Amy herself. In theory that sounds good, but in reality, even mature mothers need help."

"Come here and hold this for me," he directed, more to distract her than to aid his progress.

As Gwen stood by him, he screwed in the support plates for the mattress. Having her so close tested every good intention he had.

"Garrett, are you sure you want Tiffany and the baby in your house?"

He didn't look up. "I told the judge that would be fine."

"I know what you told the judge. That doesn't mean it's going to work...for *you.*"

Straightening, his eyes locked to hers. "Am I going to feel as if I'm getting a kick in the gut when the baby cries? Probably. Am I going to see Tiffany caring for that child and imagine what it would have been like if my marriage had worked out? Certainly. But I'm also a practical man."

"When you search for children, what do you think about?" she asked softly.

Uh-oh. She was gearing up for one of those soul-deep conversations. "I don't *think.* I *search.*"

Deciding this was a good time, he turned on the electric screwdriver and the buzz interrupted them.

When he'd finished, Gwen took the tool from his hand. "What do you think about when you search for a child?" she repeated.

"All right," he growled angrily—frustrated with

Gwen because she was disturbing his peace again. "I try to imagine what's in the kid's mind. Then I visualize bringing him or her home. Satisfied now?"

"Why do my questions make you angry?"

He really didn't have a temper. He couldn't and do the work he did. Usually when he felt anger rising up, he let it slip into a deep freeze. There he could contain it, control it and pack it away.

Before it could get to that place, Gwen clasped his wrist. "Don't disappear on me, Garrett. Tell me about this."

The anger couldn't find a place, couldn't find a sub-zero temperature and pressed like a lump in his chest with no place to land. It turned into pain.

"Tell me," she whispered. "Tell me what you're feeling."

Closing his eyes against her compassion and caring face, he took a deep breath. "I already told you I feel guilty as hell. I lost that baby for us as surely as if I'd pushed Cheryl down the stairs."

Gwen didn't protest or tell him he was wrong. Because if she had, he would have cut this off. Instead, she just stood there holding the crib, looking as if she wanted to hold him. That got to him more than anything.

"I wanted that baby. I liked the idea of being a father. Yet I also knew if we had a child, I should quit FBI work. Deep down I didn't want to do that. When Cheryl first found out she was pregnant, she told me she wanted me to be totally involved. She wanted me to help her read the baby bedtime stories, put his tooth under the pillow for the tooth fairy. She wanted me to be by her side the first day we took him to preschool. I couldn't promise her I'd be there. My job became even more of a wedge between us."

Now Gwen asked, "It meant more to you than your family?"

She wasn't accusing him of anything, he realized. She just wanted to know.

"I don't know how to explain it. You're a nurse practitioner. You're involved in your work, and I see that you enjoy it. You go out of your way to help your patients. You want to help girls like Tiffany. But…" He stopped for effect. "You're separate from what you do. Being a nurse practitioner doesn't define who you are. My job defined who I was."

Her face took on a puzzled look. "I don't understand."

They were at the bottom now and he might as well give her the rest. "When I was nine, I had a friend who was kidnapped and never found."

"Oh, Garrett." She seemed to be searching her memory for anything like that happening in Wild Horse Junction. Then she remembered. "His name was Cliff Barstow."

"That's right. Law enforcement and search parties went looking for weeks…months…and never found him."

"That had to be awful for his family…and for you."

"I so desperately wanted to be older, able to drive, able to search on my own. I figured if I had been older, if I'd been on the team looking for him, maybe it would have made a difference. I don't know why. You know how kids think. But from that moment on, I knew what kind of work I wanted to do. My parents' marriage wasn't a happy one. They fought a lot. My dad would go flying to escape. After he and I moved to California, I started taking lessons. There was such a freedom being up there that I understood my dad better. I understood myself better and my future seemed to fall into place. I went to college, worked a few years as a cop then went into training with the FBI."

He shook his head as he remembered exactly how all of it had progressed. "I became the investigator, the protector, the rescuer. That's who I was."

"So why did you get married?"

Running his hand up and down the back of his neck, he felt the tension that this conversation was causing. "I loved Cheryl as much as I knew how to love. She needed me in that big a-woman-needs-a-man sense. I spent Christmas with her family. We took a vacation together. She met my mom when my mother came to visit me. Marriage just seemed to be the way to go, although I had no idea how my marriage commitment would clash with my work, and Cheryl had every expectation in the world that I would change."

After a moment of letting everything he told her settle in, she asked, "If I tell you it wasn't all your fault, you're not going to believe me, are you?"

"No."

Now she clasped his arm, as if the gesture might make a difference. "I'm going to say it anyway. It wasn't all your fault. If you had been older, if your ex-wife had been different—"

"If the sky had been purple and the grass red."

"You're a different man now."

"No, I'm not. I changed what I do, but I'm not a different man."

"Do you really want to be alone for the rest of your life?"

Oddly enough, he could see Gwen wasn't asking the question about the two of them. It was about him. He was more uncomfortable with that than if she'd asked for a list of the women he'd slept with.

Drawing away from her, he laid down the section of the crib he'd been working on and picked up the third side. "I'm not going to be alone. Tiffany and Amy will probably be taking over my office. Hand me that screwdriver, will you? I just realized once I get this thing put together, I should buy one for my place."

"You're shutting down the conversation."

"Nope, I'm just moving it along."

He wasn't in the habit of reexamining his life. He didn't like the fact that when he was around Gwen, the reexamination happened all too easily.

Amy began crying again and Gwen glanced over her shoulder as if torn between going and staying.

"Go help Tiffany," he encouraged her. "She might want to do things on her own, but she has to learn from someone."

As Gwen stood in the doorway, looking pretty and sexy and all too caring, his heart pounded, but he ignored the primitive signals coursing through his body.

She said, "I'm glad you told me what you did."

A cynical reply came to his lips, but he kept it to himself. Often silence was the best response of all.

However, Gwen's eyes were too knowing as she finally turned and left the room.

Garrett felt as if their conversation had been more intimate than having sex.

Sex was definitely easier and a lot more fun.

Chapter Nine

"I wish my mother was like you," Tiffany murmured.

They'd just finished supper and Gwen took a good look at the teenager now. Her eyes were swimming with tears.

At the coffeepot to refill his mug Garrett shrugged, letting Gwen know he had no idea what this was about.

Throughout the afternoon and meal, Tiffany had seemed to be growing more comfortable with Garrett. He had engaged her in conversation whenever he could and Gwen knew he might claim to be a recluse, but he had more than adequate people skills. She had the feeling he could cajole rain from a cloud in the midst of a severe drought.

Now he crossed to Tiffany's side and capped her shoulder. "What's wrong?"

Beside her, Gwen encouraged her, too. "What's upsetting you?"

Tiffany turned to Gwen. "You made supper as if this was no big deal…as if you'd planned it all week. Even if my mom had let me in the house, she would have been complaining because the baby was crying, put out because there was an extra guest…" Tiffany nodded to the bundt cake on the counter. "And she never would have made dessert, too."

Gwen wrapped an arm around her. "I grew up having to expect the unexpected because my dad drank. I tried to be ready for anything. That's just carried over into the way I live now. Maybe after your mom gets used to the idea of being a grandmother, she'll come around."

Tears swam in Tiffany's eyes again as she shook her head. "She's just not like that. She doesn't want me around if it means more work."

When Gwen lifted Tiffany's chin, she gazed steadily into her eyes. "I don't look on you and Amy as more work. You're enlarging my family and I like that."

As Tiffany gave Garrett a sideways glance, she admitted, "I'm afraid I'm not going to be able to do what you want me to do. What if I mess things up for you?"

"My office is already in a mess. That's why I need you. We'll sort it out together. I won't leave you stranded on your own, until you know what you're doing."

Tiffany's face filled with emotion again, and she mumbled, "I'm going to check on Amy before I have dessert." Then she slipped away from the two of them, down the hall to the bedroom.

"I could shake her mother's bones," Gwen muttered.

Garrett closed what little distance there was between them.

"But instead, you're going to take care of her daughter and her granddaughter as if they were yours."

When Gwen gave a little shrug, she looked toward the bedroom. "She needs to have her self-esteem built up. She's a natural with Amy, but after things calm down a bit, I'll suggest she take the parenting course at the high school."

"You're going to have trouble letting go."

Although Tiffany and Amy would be happy with Gwen for a little while, she as well as Garrett knew the purpose of this was to instill independence in Tiffany and the capability of making a life for her and her daughter.

"I've been practicing letting go all of my life," Gwen quipped. "I'm good at it."

"That's what you'd like people to believe," Garrett said, his voice low. "But every time someone left, part of you got a little more broken. Did you ever think about why you chose a fiancé who didn't have staying power?"

Initially her temper wanted to retort that Garrett didn't know what he was talking about. However, over and over again she had thought about what had happened between her and Mark.

"I chose Mark because he was a good man. He was a physical therapist and we had to consult on one of my patients. He cared about the people he treated. We were in the same kind of profession and I kept telling myself we were a good match."

"Why did you have to tell yourself that? Why didn't you *know* it?"

"There was little excitement, very little surprise, lots of predictability," she admitted, standing and clearing the plates instead of meeting Garrett's eyes.

"What about sizzle?"

She stopped moving and faced the man who had made her feel the real meaning of sizzle. "That's the thing. We became friends and had to work at the sizzle. I liked Mark as a person and I knew in life there were trade-offs. I thought we could make a good life together."

"But he didn't?"

"The truth is, after we broke up, I wondered if he was still in love with the woman he dated before me. Maybe he decided what we had was less than what *they* had. They're married now."

"He just didn't show up at the wedding?"

"He called me on my cell phone when I was in my wedding gown on Dad's arm, ready to walk down the aisle. Shaye heard the tones from the little dressing room we had used. She and Kylie were both going to stand up for me."

"Were you shocked when he called?"

"I was shocked that he waited till that moment to call. As far as cutting off our engagement—well, as I said, I'm used to people walking away. I figure there must be something wrong with me." The words had tumbled out of her lips, because she'd thought them so many times.

In a moment Garrett was before her, slipping his hand into her hair. "No, Gwen. There's nothing wrong with you. Sometimes we can see patterns and think the results are our fault. Sometimes fate is just downright mean."

Could he be right? Her real parents hadn't known her

when they'd abandoned her. Had that abandonment set the course for everything that had happened after? Why had her adopted mother wanted to stop being her mother? Why couldn't her dad see that he had a child who needed him?

"Your dad hasn't walked away," Garrett reminded her.

"He might as well have. When he was out cold on the sofa when I came home from school, I didn't feel as if I had *any* parents."

"He's sober now. He's here now. I get the feeling he wants to be the father he couldn't be before."

"You've talked about this with him?"

"No. But we *did* talk at the barn dance."

"He has regrets?"

"A man doesn't get to be his age without some regrets."

Gwen already knew a lot about *Garrett's* regrets.

At the sound of footsteps, Gwen caught sight of Tiffany carrying Amy through the living room.

Reaching the kitchen, Tiffany gave her a smile. "She was awake. I thought I'd bring her in to join us while we had dessert. Or should I have left her in her crib?"

Gwen stepped away from Garrett and the pleasure of standing so close to him...being touched by him. "There aren't any rules on that one. I think we should enjoy her while she's happy and content."

As Tiffany slipped into a chair, holding her little girl as if she was the most wonderful bundle in the whole world, Gwen was once again reminded how much she wanted a little one of her own in her arms. And she wanted Garrett to be the father.

* * *

"I'll check on her," Gwen told Tiffany at the end of the reality show they'd been watching.

Garrett had sat on the floor in the living room, putting together Amy's play saucer while Gwen and Tiffany had commented on and watched the new TV program. Even though they were using a baby monitor, during every commercial, Tiffany had hopped up and gone to the baby's bedroom—just to look at her daughter and make sure she was okay.

Gwen offered now because she needed to stretch her legs. She needed some distance from Garrett. She'd kept one eye on the program and one eye on him. Every once in a while, she'd caught him glancing at her. It was as if they had an invisible string tied from her heart to his. He probably wouldn't agree with that. Even so, along that string, need and hunger vibrated back and forth until she didn't know if she was feeling his or hers.

Escaping, she slipped quietly into the bedroom and went to the crib. Amy's hair, what little she had of it, was the same color as her mother's. Her little face was round and her nose turned up at the end. In her pink sleeper, her chest rising and falling, she looked so precious. Amy gripped Gwen's heart in a way no one else ever had.

"Still sleeping?" Garrett asked, carrying in the saucer and sitting it near the changing table Gwen had borrowed from Shaye.

"Still sleeping," she murmured as he came to stand beside her at the crib, their shoulders brushing.

When she glanced at him, the shadows in the room couldn't hide the look of pain on his face.

"It hurts for you to be around her, doesn't it?"

"Like a toothache. It'll go away eventually."

"More like a heartache," she murmured. "What makes you think it will go away?"

"I'm hoping being around Amy and Tiffany will make me forget the rest."

When he lifted his hand, she saw the glow of his watch as he checked it. "I've got to get going."

"Late date?" she asked lightly.

"Late appointment over at The Silver Dollar. Clint needs advice on a new security system. He wanted to wait to consult about it until after all the help was gone."

"I see. We haven't talked about when Tiffany will start working for you. She has to be comfortable handling Amy on her own. I'm taking a vacation day tomorrow to give her a hand. I'll leave her alone for a couple hours in the afternoon so hopefully she can get used to the feeling that Amy's depending only on her."

"That's got to be scary...being a new mother," Garrett said with a shake of his head. "When she does start, I'll make sure I'm around the first few days or so. Not that I'm going to be much use."

Gwen had her own ideas on that. She had the feeling that once Garrett held the baby in his arms, he wouldn't be awkward like other men.

"Why don't we wait until Monday for her to start?" he suggested. "I'm going out of town tomorrow and don't know exactly when I'll be back—Saturday or Sunday probably."

"Is this search-and-rescue or business?"

"Business. I'm flying to D.C."

Gwen knew D.C. wasn't far from Northern Virginia where his ex-wife lived.

Her questions or curiosity must have been evident because he explained, "I've bid on a government contract to develop software. That's really all I can say."

"Do you do much of that kind of thing?"

"I did work for them once before."

After another look at Amy, he turned to Gwen. "I'll call you when I get back, then we can decide what Tiffany needs to bring along for the baby."

"All Amy will need now is the crib, diapers and plenty of formula."

As if he couldn't keep from touching Gwen, he toyed with one of her curls with his index finger. "You might not get much sleep in the next couple of months."

"I'll survive," she said gamely. When she thought of a bed and Garrett in the same sentence, sleep wasn't part of it.

"You talk a good game," he murmured as he bent closer. "But after two weeks of no sleep, you'll be singing a different song."

She couldn't think of the words to any song right now as Garrett bent his head and covered her lips with his. When he kissed her, the usual fireworks blotted out everything else. Her whole body came alive as his tongue danced with hers, as his hands hugged her waist and slid up close to her breasts.

Breaking the kiss, he murmured, "I want to take you to bed but you have chaperones."

Even in the aftermath of desire unfulfilled, she managed, "And you're glad of that, aren't you?"

As he rested his chin on her head, he folded his arms around her. "Gwen, I'm not sure *what* to do with you."

That made her push away from him. Her hands went to her hips. "Well, if you're not sure, then you don't deserve me."

He laughed. "Isn't that the truth."

When he leaned back, his smile slipped away. "You walked into my backyard and my life began to change. I'm still not sure I like it."

Halfway to the hall he stopped and turned around. "But damn it all, I like *you.*"

As she heard his bootsteps in the hall, Gwen knew her feelings for Garrett went much deeper than his for her. But with that last acerbic statement, she understood there was more than attraction between them…and so did he.

She smiled down at Amy and repeated, "He likes me."

That was enough for now.

The following afternoon, Gwen ended up in the barn at Saddle Ridge with Kylie.

"Do you spend every spare moment in here?" Gwen asked Kylie as her friend watched her new young mustang from inside the barn. The corral outside the barn door, once a large one, had been sectioned off with an extra line of fence. It was about twenty by twenty with boards encircling the top and bottom. The Bureau of Land Management had requirements for an adoption site so the horse could stay in the corral or take shelter in a twelve-by-twelve-foot box stall in the barn.

"I don't have many spare moments," Kylie answered. "Some of them I spend with Molly. Her mother is dropping her off after school so she can see the progress I'm making with Feather. Molly loves horses almost as much as I do."

Molly was a ten-year-old who'd received the gift of riding lessons from her parents for Christmas. She didn't have a horse of her own and she loved coming to Saddle Ridge whenever she could.

"You're not still giving her riding lessons, are you?"

"No. We stopped in August. I told her after the baby's born, she can continue if she wants. She said her mom might take them, too. She's such a joy to be around and good company. When her mom needs a sitter, I don't mind watching her."

This afternoon, Gwen had wanted to give Tiffany a few hours alone with Amy. She'd gravitated toward Saddle Ridge to check on her friend. Kylie's tummy was definitely growing rounder under her oversized sweatshirt.

Gwen studied the sorrel mustang in the corral. "How old is she?"

"About ten months. Isn't she a beauty? I can't wait to braid that mane."

The mare's mane and tail were flaxen.

Instead of telling her friend she had to be careful, Gwen asked, "And when do you think that's going to happen?"

"I'm not sure. She's doing well. Dix can lead her by her halter into the stall now, and she's eating out of my hand."

She took what looked like an oatmeal cookie from her pocket. "Shaye and Dylan stopped out over the weekend.

I think Dylan's goal is to repair all my fence before winter sets in. He'll become a rancher if he doesn't watch it."

Gwen could remember when Dylan wasn't sure he wanted to stay in Wild Horse Junction. "Have you been to their new house yet?"

"No, I haven't had a chance. Shaye's told me all about it, though. She's so happy she can't see straight."

"They are made for one another, even though it didn't seem like it on the surface."

Feather came trotting into the barn, stopped, cautiously eyed Gwen and proceeded toward her mistress. Kylie laughed, a sweet free sound Gwen hadn't heard in a long time. She held out the snack to the horse and Feather gobbled it up then tolerated a pat on the nose before hightailing it out to the corral again.

"Where's Dix?" Gwen asked.

"The North Ridge, moving some cattle."

When Kylie bit her lower lip, Gwen could tell there was something she wanted to talk about. Leaning against the stall, Gwen waited.

"I went through Alex's closet. The church is having a Thanksgiving drive so it seemed like a good time to do it."

"You should have called me. I would have helped you."

Kylie shook her head. "I had to do it myself. He had a few shirts from when we were first married, and I…" Her voice caught. "I kept two of them. One he wore on our honeymoon when we drove to Bozeman. The other one…" she shrugged "was one of his favorites."

"I bet lots of memories came rushing back."

Staring outside at Feather, Kylie nodded. "Yes,

they did. I had to go through everything, pockets and all that."

The hairs on Gwen's nape stood up at the change in Kylie's voice. "Pockets can be personal."

Kylie reached into her back pocket and drew out something white. "I found this."

As Gwen took the cocktail napkin, she saw it was printed with the name of Clementine's Saloon, a night spot in Wild Horse Junction.

"Turn it over," Kylie directed her.

On the back side of the napkin, in an obviously feminine flourishing cursive handwriting, Gwen read— *Alex, meet me at midnight and we'll have some fun.*

"I can't tell if it's signed with a T or an F." Gwen studied her friend. "What are you thinking?"

"You know what I'm thinking. I just don't know whether to pursue it or not."

"You mean find out who *T* or *F* is?"

Kylie nodded.

Gwen was all for the truth, but Kylie had to get on with her life now. "What good would it do to find out?"

"I could get a few questions answered."

"If you did see this woman, and if you found out for sure Alex had been unfaithful, how would that affect you? You've suspected an affair for a long time. Wouldn't it be better to concentrate on what's ahead of you, rather than what's behind you?"

Retrieving the napkin from Gwen, Kylie returned it to her pocket. "I know you're right. But when the chores are done and I can't sleep, I lay there and wonder."

"After the baby's born, you're going to be so tired all you'll want to do is sleep when you lie down."

"You're so practical," Kylie said with a small smile.

"You know being practical is just a small part of it." She encircled her friend's shoulders. "You've got to look ahead."

"It's hard looking ahead, Gwen, when I'm not meeting expenses. I can't lose this place. It's my baby's legacy and I'm afraid if I can't get it in shape, at some point Brock's going to push me to sell it."

"Do you think he'd do that?"

"I don't know what Brock would do. It's been a long time since I've seen him, even longer since we've had more than a stilted conversation. I'm writing up an ad campaign for spring, after the baby's born. It would be a good time of the year to take on two-year-olds to train. Once I get that money flowing again, maybe I can turn things around."

Kylie had to start somewhere, but Gwen had a feeling that the financial problem Saddle Ridge faced was big and Kylie wouldn't be able to take on enough horses to fix it.

"You still haven't found out if you're carrying a boy or a girl?"

"Nope. I don't want to know. I want to be surprised. I found an antique cradle in the attic. Dix brought it down for me and I cleaned it up. I just have to pick up a mattress for it. I've been sewing sheets, making little kimonos, and adding inserts to my jeans so I can wear them longer."

"When do you have time to sew?"

"I can't do as much of the physical work as I used to, so I sew instead. I'm just afraid Dix is getting overburdened. He doesn't complain but I worry about him. Dylan's helped a lot but I don't want to impose on him, either. Somehow I have to bring in more money.

Kylie wanted to take on the burden of Saddle Ridge on her own very small shoulders, but Gwen had the suspicion that if Brock Warner knew the condition the ranch was in, he'd interfere in her life whether she liked it or not.

Garrett wasn't sure why he was doing this—meeting his ex-spouse for lunch.

The Trellis hadn't changed much in the past five years. There were still photographs of the historic buildings around D.C. on the walls and an atmosphere that said everyone with briefcases was doing important work. The restaurant-goers had thinned by two in the afternoon as Garrett waited for Cheryl in the lobby.

When she walked in the door in a brown trench coat, her chin-length blond hair swinging toward her mouth, her blue eyes finding him instantly, he felt…regret. So much regret. Then he noticed her figure as she walked. Something was different. Her trench coat was open and he could see the slight protrusion under her top.

Holy thunder, she was pregnant!

The first minute was awkward, as he didn't know exactly what to say, and she didn't seem to know what to do. Then she gave him a loose hug and kissed him on the cheek. "It's good to see you."

He simply said, "I see congratulations are in order."

Her smile dimmed a bit. "We'll talk over lunch."

Once they were seated and given menus, Cheryl

shrugged out of her coat and let it fall on the back of her chair. "You're looking well. And very civilized. Not at all like a cowboy from Wyoming."

He'd worn a navy suit and tie today for his meetings. "I'm here on business. But I tucked in jeans and boots to wear on the flight home."

The smile that seemed a bit forced to him faded as she set aside her menu. "I'm so glad we could meet like this instead of talking on the phone. I never thought you'd be on the East coast again."

When he'd finally gotten hold of her his first night in D.C., she'd asked if they could talk over lunch.

Her lashes lowered, then she looked up at him. "Are you happy, Garrett?"

"Close to it." He thought about Gwen and that brought a surge of happiness that surprised him.

"I called you because everything seemed…unfinished between us. Do you know what I mean?"

"We were both hurt and angry and disillusioned."

"I said things I shouldn't have."

"Like you'd never forgive me?"

"Yes. Now that I'm pregnant again and past the first trimester, I realized I only said that to hurt you, not because it was true."

"I think you meant it when you said it."

Her eyes filled with the memories of her miscarriage, the sadness and grief that had gone along with it. "Yes, I guess I did. But I want you to know I don't blame you anymore. It was something that happened. I had to tell you that. I wasn't meant to carry that baby."

His baby. And now she was carrying someone else's. He glanced down at her hand. There was no wedding ring.

She saw his look. "I'm not married. Not yet. We're supposed to get married the beginning of December."

Something in her voice alerted him to her use of a particular word. "*Supposed* to get married?"

"Tell me something, Garrett. Why do you think we didn't work?"

Careful, man, he told himself. *This could be a minefield.*

As if sensing his hesitancy, she prompted, "Be honest. I need you to be honest."

"We didn't work for lots of reasons. First of all, I didn't know what a marriage should be. My dad was never around. I knew that played a part in my parents' divorce, but there was more to their breakup, too. Do you know what I mean? I thought as long as I took care of you the best I could, brought in a paycheck, had sex regularly, that's what marriage was."

"That was very different from what I expected… from what my parents had. They never went anywhere without each other. I don't think they've ever been separated overnight! My expectations were so different from yours."

"And now, apparently, you're engaged. To the right man?"

Her face reddened slightly. "The truth is, I don't know. I've only known him for six months. I wanted…I wanted a baby badly. He and I seemed to click. I think we're both ready for a family."

"But?"

"I'm having doubts about how fast I jumped into

this. No doubts about the baby. But as each day goes by and the wedding date gets closer, I think about our divorce and how tough it was. I think about the night you left."

"You're getting cold feet."

"It's more than cold feet. Sometimes I wake up in a full-blown panic."

Just like when they were married, Cheryl wanted him to make everything better. He hadn't known how to do that then, and he didn't know how to do it now. "Why did you want to see me?"

She looked embarrassed. "Maybe I thought you'd have some words of wisdom. Maybe I thought if we finally settled everything between us, I could move on easily."

"There's nothing between us now, unless you're still holding resentment, which I wouldn't blame you for."

Vigorously she shook her head. "No. No resentment anymore. I just—I'm not sure what to do. I want a marriage like my parents have, and I don't know if Dennis can give that to me."

"Cheryl, this Dennis won't be able to give it to you. The two of you will have to work on it together. And chances are, it won't be exactly like your parents have. Have you talked to him about this?"

"I don't want to hurt him. I don't want him to think I don't have feelings for him. I do. I just don't know if they're deep enough and strong enough."

"Then don't get married."

Her gaze lifted to his. "Not even for the sake of the baby?"

"Especially not for the sake of the baby. That baby

needs two people who know they're doing the right thing. Wait a few months until after the baby's born. Wait six months. Wait until both of you know that what you're doing is right."

The waitress came over to their table then, and a bit flustered, Cheryl opened her menu.

In that moment, Garrett knew she had always expected him to be a father figure, as well as a husband. She'd expected answers from him he couldn't always give. She'd expected a kind of love he had never understood.

Although he looked down at his menu, he saw Gwen's face. He liked her independence and her spunk and the way she talked back to him when she didn't agree.

Gwen and Cheryl were two very different women. He suddenly missed Gwen and was looking forward to seeing her again. Soon.

"How did it go today?" Gwen asked Garrett as they stood in her kitchen.

When Garrett had returned from D.C. last night, he'd called. They'd made arrangements for Gwen to drop off Tiffany and Amy today over her lunch break. He'd generously offered to bring them home at the end of the day.

"She's a good worker, and Amy cooperated by sleeping about two and a half hours this afternoon."

"You stuck around the house?"

"I worked on my laptop in the kitchen. Tiffany caught on to the computer program I use almost right away."

Gwen heaved a sigh of relief. "I'm glad. She seems comfortable with Amy now, too, as comfortable as a new mother can get."

"She picks her up every time she cries. I told her not to worry about keeping her quiet on my account."

"I think she just likes to hold her."

Silence fell between them and Gwen asked him what she hadn't asked him last night when he called. "So how did your trip go?"

Leaning against the counter, he crossed his arms over his chest and she took it for the defensive gesture it was. "It went fine."

"When will you know if you got the contract?"

"I'm not sure."

"Obviously you don't want to talk about it."

"I *can't* talk about it."

Garrett was the tall, dark and silent type. It was the silent part that was frustrating. He must have realized that because he took her hand and pulled her close.

"Does it matter?" he asked.

"I suppose not." He had shared a lot with her about his background and about his ex-wife. He had shared what mattered. That should be enough.

But will he share his heart, his soul and his life? a wise little voice asked.

Bending his forehead to hers, he touched noses with her and wrapped her tighter into his arms. She felt a rightness when their bodies touched like this. Excitement began its tingling journey through her as his lips hovered over hers.

He whispered, "I missed you."

He began a kiss that had seemed much too long in coming. No matter what he'd been doing in D.C., he'd admitted he missed her and she had missed him. She had thought about him way too much as she tried to figure out what their relationship meant to her life. She loved him. She was beginning to see a future for them. But he was right about her—wedding veils were in her dreams, and he'd made it clear that marriage wasn't in his life picture. Not again.

Instead of kissing her outright, he took tiny nibbles at the corners of her lips. Questions fled as she laced her hands into his hair and parted her lips. As always when Garrett kissed her, her world spun, her body sang, her mind gave up trying to figure anything out as pleasurable sensation whirled around her. His hands tunneled under the hem of her sweater until his fingers met her midriff. She shivered from the erotic thrill of his hands spanning her waist.

He broke the kiss once, looked deep into her eyes, then came back for more. As she responded freely, she felt him letting his guard drop, letting his hunger increase, letting their passion explode.

Yet seconds later, she realized Garrett always maintained control. Although his fingers were still scorching hot on her skin as he held her, he slowed down their passion and backed away from their desire. His lips clung to hers reluctantly as if he didn't want to pull away.

Yet he did.

"Tiffany will probably be finished feeding Amy pretty soon."

Gwen knew he was right. She knew they had to be practical. She knew she had a single mom and a baby to think of now, rather than just herself.

Taking a breath to try to right her world, knowing her

world wouldn't be right unless Garrett was in it, she asked, "Do you want to stay for supper?"

"I'd like that."

Old fears gnawed at Gwen, reminding her lots of people had walked away from her. A hopeful voice in her heart whispered, *This time will be different.*

She clung to that belief.

Chapter Ten

Gwen had just finished with a patient on Thursday when the receptionist buzzed her. Tiffany was on the line. "Garrett had to go out of town. Can you pick me up?" she asked.

"Sure. I'll be there around five."

Since Monday, Gwen had been asking herself, *What did Garrett feel?*

That was the million-dollar question. Since Monday, they hadn't spent any time alone. Maybe because they knew if they did they'd end up in bed…because she and Garrett were dry kindling just waiting for a random spark to ignite them.

He'd joined them for supper every night. When they were all together, they felt like a family.

After Gwen finished talking to Tiffany, she tried to call her dad to see if he wanted to join them for supper. The first time he'd met Tiffany and Amy, he'd been a bit bemused by the fact that his daughter had taken in a perfect stranger. But then he'd seemed to fit into a grandfatherly role, even holding the baby. He'd probably enjoy a home-cooked meal tonight instead of warming a TV dinner in the microwave.

But Gwen couldn't get hold of him, and that was odd. He had a cell phone now and because of his work, he usually kept it with him. Maybe it wasn't charged. Maybe it was in his car. Maybe—

No. There was no reason for him to be drinking again.

Alcoholics don't need a reason to drink, the voice of experience told her.

What we fear, we create, Garrett had said.

She wouldn't go there. Just because she couldn't reach her dad didn't mean he was drinking.

However, when she tried again at three and then once more before leaving work, she was truly worried.

When Gwen picked up Tiffany, the young mother could see she was troubled.

"What's wrong?" she asked as she fastened her seat belt. "Did someone from family services call? Is there a problem?"

Underlying the words, Gwen could read the questions Tiffany really wanted to ask. *Do you want me and Amy to move somewhere else? Are we too much of a bother? Will you toss us out like my mother did?*

Quickly she reached across the seat and patted Tiffany's hand. "There isn't a problem. At least not with you and Amy. I might be worrying for nothing, but I can't get hold of Dad."

Before her father had come for breakfast the Saturday after Tiffany and Amy had moved in, she'd told Tiffany more fully about her childhood, her dad's alcoholism and his current sobriety.

"Do you think he might be at Clementine's?" Tiffany asked, wide-eyed. "Do you want to stop by and check?"

Glancing over her shoulder at Amy, Gwen decided, "I'll take you home first."

"Sure you don't want someone with you?"

Gwen wanted to hug Tiffany for her offer. "Thanks, but I'll do this on my own."

"You don't know what you'll find," Tiffany said wisely.

"I don't know what I'll find," Gwen agreed, not wanting Tiffany to have to deal with any more than she already had. Gwen didn't want to face the possibilities herself, but she had no choice.

A short time later, darkness shattered only by the streetlamp, Gwen parked in front of her family home—the home she'd known as a child, the home she'd escaped from when she was able. As a teenager, first on her bike, then in the rattletrap car she'd managed to save up to buy, she'd spent a lot of time at Kylie's. Kylie's dad had often been gone a few days at a time, chasing the thrills of a rodeo, just like Alex had.

Was it true girls tended to marry men like their fathers?

Gwen sincerely hoped not.

Walking up the porch steps, Gwen told herself she was prepared for anything. She knocked first, then rang the bell, hoping her dad had just had his phone turned off, had been napping. Something.

No one answered the door. It was open, though. Her dad never locked his doors.

Inside the house that now saw a dusting and vacuuming by a cleaning lady once a month, she noticed the natural disorder of a bachelor living alone—magazines tossed here and there, slippers beside the recliner, a half-read newspaper open on the sofa.

"Dad," she called, hoping for an answer. Maybe *not* hoping for an answer.

The stairs loomed ahead of her. She didn't want to climb those steps to the bedroom. She didn't want to find her father passed out. She didn't want her hopes dashed again.

Yet she straightened her back and climbed the steps anyway. Never had she worn blinders as far as her dad's drinking was concerned, and she wouldn't start now. She knew she couldn't evade reality.

Flipping on the hall light, she mounted the stairs and stood at the top, peering into her father's room. The bed was made…and it was empty.

The relief that swept over her was almost overwhelming. She knew she shouldn't be relieved. He could still be at Clementine's. He could still be somewhere else with a fifth of vodka in front of him.

Before she could turn around and decide what to do next, she heard the front door open and her dad call, "Gwen? Are you here?"

Hurrying downstairs, she stopped in the foyer to examine her father. He was smiling. His eyes were sparkling. He was wearing jeans, a sweatshirt and an all-weather jacket.

"Where have you been?" she asked, trying to keep her tone tempered. "You didn't answer your cell phone or this one." She gestured toward the cordless in the living room.

"Do you want me to take a Breathalyzer?" he asked, his voice serious, the twinkle gone from his eyes.

He looked clear-eyed, and well, not like a man who'd been drinking one shot after another. "I was worried. I called to invite you to dinner, and when I couldn't find you—" she broke off.

"You thought the worst, as you usually do. As I've taught you to do. I'm sorry, Gwen. I'm sober. In fact, I'm more than sober. I was with Garrett. We went on a search-and-rescue mission."

She now noticed there were binoculars in her dad's hand. As she followed him into the living room, he took off his jacket and tossed it over the sofa. "With Garrett? Since when?"

"We had a talk at the barn dance. Afterward, I called him and asked if he needed a spotter. I'd like something in my life besides work. It just seemed like a good idea."

"Garrett thought so, too?"

"He wasn't sure. He told me he had to think about it. Then today he got a call and he called me. This could be what I've been looking for. Just hanging around his plane makes me feel…worthwhile again."

"Garrett didn't tell me you called him."

"I asked him not to. Not until he made a decision. I knew you'd think it was just another pipe dream of mine. You know, Gwen, at some point you're going to have to have faith in me to stay sober. You're going to have to have faith in me that I can make my life *mean* something."

"And you really think being a spotter for Garrett can do that?"

Her father shoved his hands into his jeans pockets. "Not on its own. But it can help. Teenagers went hiking today and got lost. We found them. In fact, *I* spotted them, then Garrett radioed in."

On one hand, Gwen was happy for her father, but she was upset that Garrett had kept this from her. It involved her *dad*, for heaven's sake.

Supper tonight was out of the question. Tiffany was probably bathing Amy and getting her ready for bed. But tomorrow night…

"I have to get home to Amy and Tiffany," she said, "but how about supper tomorrow night? I'll put something in the Crock-Pot before I leave for work. Then you can tell us all about searching for those teenagers."

"Sounds good to me." Her father looked pleased at her invitation and the fact she wanted to hear about his adventure. "Maybe some night soon I can invite Dorothy along and we can all go someplace to eat."

Over the years her father hadn't dated much. "You've seen her since the barn dance?"

"We caught a movie last weekend. She's a nice lady."

His life *was* changing. "All right. You find out what nights are good for her, then let me know."

Crossing to her dad, Gwen gave him a hug. "The next time you do something like today, can you call me and let me know?"

"Things happened so fast today, I didn't even think about calling you. But yeah, I'll try to do that. And can you not push the panic button as soon as you can't get hold of me?"

Leaning away from him, she stared into his clear blue eyes. "I'll try to hold off pushing the panic button."

A few minutes later as Gwen sat in her van outside of her father's house, mixed emotions swirled inside of her. *Could* she give her dad the benefit of the doubt? *Could* she trust him to run his own life? To stay sober?

Taking her cell phone from her purse, she brought up Garrett's name in her address book and hit the number.

He answered on the second ring.

"Garrett, it's Gwen."

"Hi, Gwen," he said cautiously, as if he knew what was coming.

"I just spent a couple of hours worrying about Dad because I couldn't get hold of him. When he got home, he told me he'd been with you. Why didn't you let me know he was interested in going up with you?" She tried to keep her voice even but the note of accusation was there.

Gwen counted five beats of silence until Garrett replied calmly, "It was up to him to tell you."

"You couldn't have said, 'Your dad's interested in going on some search-and-rescue trips with me?' What would have been the harm in that? It's not like it was some big secret, was it?"

"Your dad preferred I *not* tell you and I respected that."

"What about your respect for me? What about our...friendship?" she settled on, not able to find a word she wanted.

"This didn't have anything to do with you and me."

"Of course it did."

"No. Your father made it clear he wanted me to make a decision independent of you."

"How could it be independent of me when you and I are—"

"I think involved is the word you're looking for. Tell me something, Gwen. If I had told you about your dad, what would you have done? Tried to talk me out of it? Tried to talk *him* out of it? Told me I was making a mistake considering it? Told *him* he should get sober on the ground instead of trying to fly?"

"I don't know what I would have done. I didn't have a chance to find out."

She heard him sigh. "You're acting like a parent with him, Gwen, and you're not. You're his daughter. You're going to have to learn to relate to him as an adult, rather than treating him like a child."

Maybe she was. And maybe she had started to tonight. But that was separate from her upset with Garrett. "I'll work it out. But what I don't know is if I can work out you keeping something like that from me."

"You're making too much of this."

"And you're not trying to understand how I feel." She realized now she shouldn't have called him. She should have gone to see him face-to-face.

"I've got to go, Gwen. My cell phone's ringing and it could be important."

She could understand his cell phone ringing. She could understand his need to go. What she couldn't understand was that she felt diminished by his attitude.

"You go, Garrett. I have a feeling you ended a lot of conversations this way with your ex-wife."

Then she clicked off.

The little window on her phone still glowed for a couple of seconds, then the light went out, and she wondered what she'd done. She'd let her hurt get the best of her. She shouldn't have said anything in anger. Maybe it hadn't been entirely fair.

Fair. Who knew what was fair anymore? She wanted to get closer to Garrett, not shove him away. But tonight that's probably what she'd done.

Switching on the ignition, she headed home.

Gwen was in the kitchen studying the contents of the refrigerator, trying to decide what she was going to toss into the slow cooker for tomorrow's supper when her doorbell rang. Checking the clock above the sink, she saw it was 11:00 p.m.

When she went to the door, she called, "Who is it?"

"It's Garrett."

Her heart began racing and she quickly unlocked the door. His expression was serious and she wondered if he'd come to tell her they weren't involved anymore.

"Have a few minutes?" he asked.

"Sure. Come on in."

Moments later they were standing in the living room and Garrett was removing his jacket. She supposed that was a good sign. Maybe. She wished she'd dressed in something other than her faded blue sweatsuit, but she'd never expected him to turn up at her door.

Gingerly she sat on the sofa with him, though not

very close. She couldn't read whether he was upset, angry or maybe neither. That was the thing about Garrett. He had to tell her what he was thinking because she could never guess.

Looking uncomfortable, he admitted, "I never should have said what I did on the phone. You and your father have to find your own way. I don't have any right to interfere or judge what you're doing."

"I shouldn't have said what *I* did."

His gaze shifted from her to the coffee table, then back to her. "You were right."

She wasn't sure what she was right about, so she kept quiet.

"A lot of my conversations with Cheryl ended because of the ring of the cell phone. Sometimes it couldn't be helped, sometimes it could. What you said made me realize work gave me an excuse not to have the kind of discussions she wanted to have. Not to face our differences. Before I went to D.C., Cheryl called me. I had lunch with her there, and I think we got old baggage cleaned up."

He saw his ex-wife in D.C? But he was telling her about it. Just so the old baggage had been cleaned up rather than reopened.

Better just to keep silent, listen and see where this led.

"I don't want to repeat the old pattern. But you've got to understand something, Gwen. I will never have a nine-to-five job. When that phone rings, if it's a business wanting my services, yeah, I can put them on hold. I can wait to take the message. I can wait to return the call. But if it's about a kid who's gone missing and can't be found, I go."

So he hadn't come to talk about his ex-wife, but rather what Gwen could accept...or couldn't. She thought carefully about his search-and-rescue trips.

"I know that you have to go."

"Do you?"

"Yes. Do *you* realize that I felt betrayed because you didn't tell me about my father?"

"Betrayed is a strong word."

"Yes, it is. But it's what I felt. I felt the same way when I realized Mark had kept things from me. He had doubts and he didn't bring them up. He realized his feelings for me weren't strong enough, and he didn't tell me."

Garrett's gaze was on her again and he shifted closer. "Men don't like to discuss. They'd rather do other things."

"Garrett—" she said with some exasperation.

Closer still, he slid his hand to her neck and pulled her to him. "I get what you're telling me. But you also have to understand I gave your dad my word."

"I understand," she admitted, knowing that was one of the qualities about Garrett she loved. He was a man of his word.

"If I kiss you," he murmured, "I'm not going to want to stop."

"There *are* disadvantages to having housemates," Gwen agreed.

"Come over to my place tomorrow night," he suggested gruffly.

"I can't. I asked Dad for supper. You can come, too."

"I need to eat. But I need to be alone with you more. What about Saturday night?"

"My calendar's free. Tiffany's doing a good job with

Amy. I have no qualms about leaving her alone longer now…just so I'm not too far away."

"I like your calendar being free. And I'm glad you trust Tiffany." His lips hovered an inch from hers. "Because you might be at my house all night. You'd better prepare her for that."

Prepare Tiffany?

Gwen had to make sure she was prepared herself. She lifted her lips to Garrett's as if she was looking forward to becoming intimate with him. She just had to wonder how intimate Garrett would let himself be with *any* woman.

Saturday night she would find out.

"Chocolate cream pie. You certainly know the way to a man's stomach."

When Garrett had told her he would make supper, Gwen had offered to bring dessert. But she really didn't care that much about winning over his taste buds. She wanted to win his heart.

"I knew you liked chocolate."

"And cream," he said with the wiggle of one brow.

She laughed. "What are we having?"

"Ribs are glazing in the slow cooker and potatoes are baking in the oven. The salad's already made in the fridge, so we're all set."

All set might mean something different for Garrett than it meant for her, and she was waiting for clarification as she took off her jacket and hung it over a chair in the breakfast nook. "It all sounds delicious." She checked her watch. "Are you hungry now?"

Garrett's jeans looked new. So did his football shirt.

With his hair falling over his forehead, he'd never looked more rugged, more sexy, more male. His gray eyes were intense tonight, with a message she hoped she understood.

"Are *you* hungry?" he returned.

Was that a loaded question! "I'm not ravenous. Did you have something else in mind?"

"I thought we could start the evening off with a soak in the hot tub. Then we could eat and let the night go wherever it wants…wherever we want to take it."

The thought of taking tonight into intimacy with Garrett made her almost giddy. Yet her picket fence dream tapped her on the shoulder. She was old enough and experienced enough to know most dreams didn't come true. But this chemistry she had with Garrett and her admiration for him came along once in a lifetime. She couldn't throw that away because she had once been hurt…or because *he* had once been hurt. Could she?

"I didn't bring a bathing suit."

"You don't need a bathing suit," he assured her. "And I have a robe you can use to get you to the tub."

"If I wear your robe, what will you wear?"

"Sweatpants, until I get to the tub."

She felt wobbly-kneed already, just at the thought of seeing Garrett naked. And he would see her naked. She was a woman of the twenty-first century. She wasn't a modest virgin, afraid of her own sexuality. Yet suddenly she did feel modest and wasn't at all sure how to handle this situation.

Garrett ambled over to her, closing the space between them. "Do you not want to soak in the hot tub naked?"

"It's not that. I just feel...self-conscious thinking about it."

"It's dark out there, Gwen. The tub's completely surrounded by cedar. The only light will come from the lamps in the bottom of the tub...unless there's a moon. I'll let you slip in first if you feel funny about disrobing in front of me."

Her cheeks were hot and she couldn't understand why this discussion was so hard for her. "That would be fine. I don't know why I'm being so...old-fashioned about this."

Encircling her with his arms, he leaned against the table and brought her between his legs. "You're an old-fashioned kind of girl whether you admit it or not. And that's okay. You're cute when you blush."

"I don't blush in front of anybody but you."

"It's good to know I'm special," he joked.

She took his face between her hands and ran her thumb over the cleft in his jaw. "You *are* special. That's why I'm here."

Now *he* looked uncomfortable. Gruffly, he suggested, "We've been working up to this for a long time."

It had been five weeks since she'd come calling on him for his help. "Since the moment we met."

The heat between their bodies was rising. His arousal was obvious as she placed a light kiss on his lips.

His arms tightened around her for an instant and then he leaned away. "We're going to stretch out this night and take pleasure in everything we do. Let's get that soak."

She hoped tonight was going to be about more than

pleasure. For her it would be about love, and giving that love to Garrett freely.

"I laid my robe on the bed in the spare room if you want to change in there."

Garrett's plan apparently wasn't to jump her bones… or to let her jump his. Maybe after the hot tub, after dinner and chocolate cream pie, after wine and kissing and touching, they'd satisfy their intense anticipation, curiosity and desire.

Garrett's spare room held a double bed with a black iron frame, a small dresser with a tilt mirror and a straight-back chair. He had filled his house with furniture he was comfortable with, not because it went together or created a mood, though it did. The ambience in the log home was rustic, almost primitive, yet with Western touches that made it all work. The only exception was his office in the loft. She hadn't seen it herself yet but Tiffany had told her about the airplane mobile and the *Return of the Jedi* poster that hung up there.

Gwen smiled at the thought.

There was a *clunk* in the room next to hers, like a belt buckle hitting the floor. How had Garrett furnished the master bedroom?

Later, she'd find out.

Garrett's robe was heavy, huge and long enough to go to her ankles. Multicolored velour, it didn't look like anything he'd buy. Maybe it had been a present from his mother. A present from his ex-wife?

Voiding that thought, tying the long belt around her waist, she fashioned it into an extra-large bow. Stepping into the hall barefooted, she wondered if she should have slipped on the black leather flats she'd worn with her slacks. But just then, Garrett emerged from his bedroom and the thought of shoes seemed inconsequential. He was wearing navy sweatpants that hung low on his hips and tied with a drawstring under his navel. That was it. No shirt. No shoes. His dark brown chest hair was thick and formed a T, the bottom of which arrowed under that drawstring.

"Are you ready?" he asked gently.

She silently nodded, unable to find her voice... unable to slow her heart...unable to saddle the anticipation running rampant inside of her.

He opened the hall closet and took out two large towels that were patterned in stripes of rust and tan.

She glanced briefly at one as Garrett handed it to her and asked, "Would you like to take the wine along, or save it until after we come in?"

"Let's wait until we come in," she suggested.

As soon as they stepped outside, Gwen knew this was an experience she wasn't going to soon forget. A breeze carried the scent of sage and pine. A light burned over the back door, and Garrett was backlit for a few moments as he pulled the door shut. The wood of the deck was cold under her feet because the temperature had dropped. She imagined snow might even be falling in the higher altitudes of the Painted Peaks. This was the high desert and she couldn't imagine ever living anywhere else.

The gazebolike structure was only twelve feet away. Garrett moved ahead of her, opened the door that led inside and handed her the towel. "I'll be there in a minute. I want to open the roof."

She watched as he went to the side of the building and climbed up a short ladder. Then he reached to the roof and she heard something unlatch. Wanting to see what it was, she stepped through the door and spotted the sunken hot tub. Lights glowed under the water and she could see the tub was teal-colored.

Looking up, she saw what Garrett had opened—a skylight to the stars. And there was a moon...a crescent moon, casting white light on everything under it. It seemed to trickle down into the tub.

Gwen knew Garrett was giving her this time to slip into the water before he came in. Before tonight, she'd touched him with his clothes on. He'd touched her naked breasts. Yet that had been so different from this.

There were hooks on the wall. Unbelting Garrett's robe, she slid it off and hung it there. When she turned to step into the tub, Garrett appeared in the doorway. Even in the shadowy enclosure, she knew his gaze was on her. She could feel it.

"Do you want me to leave for a few minutes until you're settled in the water?"

That's what she'd thought she'd wanted. But with Garrett here, looking at her like that, she changed her mind. "I don't need a few minutes."

Unabashedly, she stepped toward the tub and descended the steps into it, knowing he was watching her every move. Once in the center of the hot tub, she faced him. "Are you going to stand there or are you going to get undressed and come in?"

With a slow, lazy smile, he pulled the drawstring on his pants and dropped them.

As she admired his beautifully aroused male body, her heart pounded fast and the beat of it echoed in her ears.

Garrett hadn't prepared himself for the impact of seeing Gwen naked. He watched spellbound as she sank down into the steaming water, her hair curling into ringlets, her shoulders creamy white, her smile a hit to his solar plexus. Taking the evening slow, treating a soak in the hot tub as foreplay had seemed to be a great idea in theory.

Now he wasn't so sure.

Descending the steps into the tub, he sat beside her.

She was looking up…not at him. "The open roof is a terrific idea. Look at that sky."

Someone had spread a star blanket above them.

"Do you come out here much?" she asked.

He had to clear his throat. He had to get a grip on desire that didn't want to be restrained. "Mostly after search-and-rescue missions. It seems as if I need it then."

They weren't touching yet, but their hips would brush if either of them took a deep breath. "Would you like me to turn the jets on?" he asked.

Gwen nodded, her brown eyes huge and sparkling.

When he pressed a button on the side of the tub, the water spurted to life, swirling all around them.

Gwen closed her eyes. "Mmm. This is nice."

He knew what would be even nicer. When he slid his arm around her, she turned into his body. He didn't want to talk, and he knew that Gwen would…if he gave her any time at all. She was a talker. He was a doer.

His lips came down on hers with the intention of

teasing, of awakening her desire slowly and saving the main course for after dinner. But once they were in each other's arms, plans changed.

He couldn't get enough of her—not enough of her lips or her tongue or her skin sliding against his. As steam rose in wisps toward the sky, as bubbles frothed around them, as damp brush and sage rode on the crisp, clean air and mingled with the tub's humidity, Garrett forgot this was supposed to be foreplay.

Before he'd realized he'd done it, he'd scooped Gwen onto his lap. "Do you know how crazy you've made me since I met you?" he asked hoarsely, as his hand skimmed her breast, settled on it and palmed her nipple.

"I never meant to make you crazy," she managed to say, sounding breathless. She wrapped one arm around his neck. Her other hand swirled through his chest hair. "You affected me, too. When you looked at me, it felt as if you could see everything I was and everything I'd ever been."

"Do you know how long it took me to get that look down?" he jibed, trying to lighten something that was growing more serious.

"Probably years. Did you practice on hardened criminals?"

"I practiced on everyone for about a year. I learned fast I had to have the upper hand. In spite of that look, and all my years of experience, with you I don't." He knew he didn't sound happy about it, and he wasn't. He wasn't used to a woman throwing him off his game, making him sidestep instead of moving forward, forcing him to rethink something he did or said.

"You still have the upper hand most of the time," she assured him with a small smile. Then she let her hand trail down, down, down until she was just below his navel.

"Damn it, Gwen," he growled, and kissed her hard, needing her in a primal way that blinded him to repercussions and consequences and a much different path to the future than any he'd contemplated. While their tongues darted around each other and settled down to explore, while the kiss went on and on, while their bodies yearned to join, Garrett lifted her so she straddled him.

They never stopped kissing—not as he gripped her buttocks and slid her forward, not as he entered her, not as she contracted tightly around him and wound her arms around his neck. The night was pure sensation as they finally broke their kiss and she slid back and forth on him in rhythm with his thrusting. This was a fantasy he'd indulged in but never expected to happen.

Discovering now that fantasies took on a life of their own, he lost all self-control and any restraint he might have possessed before he set foot in the tub. He let go of years of telling himself he didn't need a woman. He released the barriers between them—Gwen's fear of abandonment, his oath that he'd never get seriously involved again. Her body welcomed him so beautifully as he found the physical satisfaction he'd been craving for months. He found ecstasy in the moment for the first time in his life.

He'd planned and investigated and analyzed for so long he'd forgotten how to live. His shout of release told the world he was alive again.

When Gwen stiffened and called his name almost simultaneously, he knew she felt the power of their sexual fulfillment, too.

His body actually shook. Hers trembled. He held her to him while the water swirled and soothed and bathed them in the fantasy of a world set apart from reality.

He wasn't sure which of them first realized exactly what had happened.

When she leaned back and gazed up at him, their eyes locked.

His words tangled with hers as they both said at the same time, "We didn't use protection."

"You aren't on the pill?" he asked, though he knew from her expression there was no point.

"I haven't been involved with anyone since…Mark."

Mark. The jerk who'd left her at the altar. The last abandonment in a long line of them.

He caught his oath before it passed his lips. "I never intended for this to happen this way. I had condoms in the bedroom. Is there such a thing as a woman's safe time? Are we anywhere close?"

"No. We're not close."

He could swear and call himself every kind of fool. He could get angry that a woman of her age and experience hadn't expected to use more protection than a thin prophylactic barrier. He had called Gwen a Pollyanna, and in some ways, she was. In others, she was as realistic as he was. They'd have to deal with reality now.

Before he could help her off his legs, she was sliding over to the bench. The lower portion of her curls were wet. She rested her head against the lip of the tub and closed her eyes.

Garrett switched off the jets. "There are two bathrooms in the house. One upstairs, off the loft, the other in the hall with the bedrooms. I'll go upstairs and shower. I'll meet you in the kitchen and we'll have supper and talk."

When she opened her eyes, she asked, "Is there anything to talk about?"

"Let's get something to eat—"

"And pretend we're enjoying the ribs? While there's a rock in your stomach as you figure out what to say to me? And there's a rock in mine because I don't want to hear what you have to say?"

It was damned disconcerting that she could read him better than anyone else in his life. "You're not going to just hop out of here and leave with your hair wet."

She hesitated only a moment. "I'll get a shower and towel off, then leave."

When she stood to go, he stood, too, and grabbed her wrist.

She looked down at it, and then up at him. "What do you want, Garrett? A simple affair in between bites of chocolate pie? We both blew the idea of that tonight."

"You might not get pregnant."

"True. Or I *might*. You haven't changed your mind, have you, hypothetically speaking of course, of wanting children and a wife as a life partner?"

"Hypothetically speaking, no, I haven't."

"Well then," she said breaking free of his grip, "that says it all."

Quicker than he'd ever seen her move, Gwen was out of the tub, into the robe and stepping onto the deck.

She'd gone inside by the time he left the hot tub enclosure. He didn't go after her. They both needed cooling down time.

While Garrett showered upstairs, he thought about her downstairs. Although he dressed quickly, by the time he'd descended the steps, he felt the emptiness in the house. She hadn't showered. She'd dressed and left with her hair wet.

The chocolate cream pie sat in the middle of his table. He wanted to put his fist through the wall.

Chapter Eleven

Was she pregnant or wasn't she?

For almost two weeks, Gwen had been pretending as if leaving Garrett's house as she had hadn't affected her. Well, it had. As much as their interlude in the hot tub. She loved Garrett, and making love with him had powerfully shown her how much. Stupidly, as soon as she'd stepped into that hot tub, all practical thoughts had left her. When he'd scooped her onto his lap she'd been lost in the moonlit night, the intimacy of steam, the scent and feel of Garrett.

Stupid, stupid, stupid.

And now, as she sat at the kitchen table, sorting bills, she knew she had to use a pregnancy test, but she was postponing doing it.

Her attention was thankfully snagged by Tiffany who came into the kitchen with Amy on her shoulder.

"All bathed?" Gwen asked.

When Tiffany had first brought Amy home, she'd wanted Gwen there to make sure she was doing things right. Especially bathing. But now she handled almost everything on her own. Gwen helped her at night if Amy had a fussy spell. But for the most part, Tiffany was handling her responsibilities and Gwen was just a doting aunt.

Her heart still ached to have her own baby, Garrett's baby. That was probably why she'd postponed using a pregnancy test—the results would fulfill her hopes or dash her dreams.

Tiffany transferred Amy to the crook of her arm and dug something out of her jeans pocket. "I wanted to give you this." She handed Gwen two twenties and a five-dollar bill.

"What's this?"

"What I had left over after buying Amy's supplies for next week. I want to start paying you back."

"Tiffany, you don't have to do that."

"I know, but I want to. I have to start taking care of everything Amy needs."

"I think you should save this for a rainy day…for an expense you don't expect. Amy will have a doctor's visit coming up soon, won't she?"

Tiffany had obviously forgotten about that. "There's always someplace for it to go, isn't there?" she asked.

"Always."

"Mr. Maxwell said once Amy starts crawling, he'll move his computer down to the spare room. Then I won't have to worry about the stairs."

Tiffany and Gwen hadn't talked about Garrett and she didn't particularly want to do it now. "Maybe we can arrange a different schedule. Possibly you could work in the evenings and I can watch her here. Then Garrett doesn't have to rearrange his house and you won't be distracted."

"You'd do that?"

Unable to help herself, Gwen stood and scooped Amy out of Tiffany's arms. She ran her finger over the cute little forehead and down the pug nose. "Of course, I'd do that."

"If I couldn't get in enough hours that way, I could always add Saturday mornings. But of course you'd be tied up then, too."

"We'll work it out."

"Did you and Mr. Maxwell mix things up? I mean, he never comes over here anymore."

"We had a difference of opinion."

"He acts like he's not interested when I bring you up, but he is."

Gwen cast Tiffany a sideways glance. "And why would you be bringing me up?"

Tiffany shrugged and grinned. "To get his reaction. I wondered what was going on. But he doesn't say anything."

That was Garrett. Gwen didn't really want to discuss her love life, or lack of it, with Tiffany. She thought she had to be a role model for her. What had happened with Garrett had been irresponsible and foolish. If she was pregnant, she'd have to tell her. But she'd wait and see.

"I'm almost finished with the bills. Do you want to watch a movie after Amy goes to bed?"

"That sounds good."

Amy started to squiggle and Tiffany took her from Gwen's arms. After she crossed to the doorway, she stopped. "Do you think Justin will ever try to find me?"

Gwen's views on Tiffany's boyfriend were about the same as her views on the girl's mother. But she kept her voice nonjudgmental. "Do you want him to find you?"

"No."

"Do you want Garrett to find *him*?"

"No," Tiffany answered with even more surety. "Not after what he did to me. I don't need a man in my life who's going to cut out and leave. If he did it once, he'll do it again."

"I think you're right about that," Gwen agreed, thinking about Garrett, knowing her situation was much different from Tiffany's. Garrett had never wanted to get involved. Neither had she, as far as that went.

A half hour later, Gwen and Tiffany were watching a Drew Barrymore flick when the doorbell rang. When Gwen glanced at Tiffany, the teenager shrugged. "Maybe it's Garrett."

Carefully Gwen set the bowl of popcorn that had been in her lap on the coffee table. "What do you know that I don't know?"

"He asked if you were going to be home tonight."

"And you didn't tell me?"

"I didn't want you to be disappointed if he didn't show."

How could she be angry about that? After all,

Tiffany was just trying to take care of her, the way she tried to protect Tiffany. Suddenly she was aware that she was wearing her old comfortable jeans with an often-washed, cowl-neck top printed with wild horses.

Reading her mind, Tiffany commented, "You look fine. Answer the door before he goes away."

Gwen wasn't so sure she didn't want him to go away.

She didn't hurry to the door because she was trying to prepare herself for seeing him again.

A lot of good *that* did. She still wasn't prepared when she opened the door and there he was in a gray leather jacket and black jeans. In his hands he held her pie plate.

"I came to return this," he said, as if that was a valid reason.

"You couldn't have given it to Tiffany?"

"I could have. But then I couldn't have told you in person how good the pie was."

She rolled her eyes. "Why did you really come tonight?" She couldn't help that kernel of hope that wanted to dig in its roots and sprout in her heart.

"I wondered if you used the pregnancy test yet. I looked it up on the Web, and you can get a valid reading after seven to ten days. It's been two weeks."

She kept her voice low. "I haven't—"

Suddenly Tiffany was by her shoulder, looking at the two of them. "He doesn't have to stand outside. Invite him in. I'll go back to my bedroom and read."

"You were watching a movie. You don't have to go anywhere," Gwen assured her.

"That's right," Garrett agreed, as he gave the pie plate

to Tiffany. "Gwen's coming out with me. Get your coat," he directed her.

Gwen gave him a look she didn't have to put into words.

With a sigh he asked, "How about coming with me? We'll stop and get the things we need, then go back to my place."

He was speaking in code for Tiffany's sake, but Gwen didn't know if she wanted to be pushed into buying a pregnancy test. Still, she should find out one way or the other what the future held.

"Go on," Tiffany urged her. "I'll watch the rest of the movie and tell you what happens…in detail."

Five minutes later, Gwen found herself beside Garrett in his SUV, neither of them saying a word, both of them sneaking glances at each other.

Finally, when they pulled up in front of a small shopping plaza and he parked at the drugstore, he said, "You shouldn't have left like that."

"I couldn't sit there and eat supper with you as if nothing had happened. As if you wanted me there."

With a quick jerk of his hand, he switched off the ignition. "I wouldn't have asked you to stay if I hadn't wanted you there."

"You felt duty-bound, Garrett. I don't want any man to be with me out of duty."

His scowl set his jaw. After a moment, he unfastened his seat belt. "You might change your mind if that test shows positive."

"I won't change my mind. *Especially* if the test shows positive." Unclasping *her* seat belt, she was out of the car and into the store before he could say anything else.

Since Gwen rushed ahead of him, Garrett stood at the door by the magazine rack, his arms crossed over his chest.

Gwen almost smiled. He was as uncomfortable about this as she was, but trying to act as if he wasn't.

Unfortunately, she recognized the girl at the cashier's desk. She was a senior at the high school. Her eyes got big and wide when she saw the pregnancy test.

Gwen just said, "It's for a friend," paid, took her package and swept out the door in front of Garrett.

Coming out right behind her he offered, "You don't lie well."

"Maybe I'll have to work on that," she tossed at him as she opened the door.

After he caught her arm, he swung her around to him. "No, you won't. One of the things I like most about you, Gwen, is your honesty."

Her chest felt tight and her eyes burned. He liked her. She knew that. But did his feelings go any deeper than that? Even if they did and he denied them, what was the point?

Pulling out of his grasp, she climbed up into the SUV.

With a frustrated expression on his usually inscrutable face, he stepped away so she could close the door.

They rode in silence to Garrett's house. Once inside, Garrett moved toward the stack of logs in the cubicle beside the fireplace. "I'm going to start a fire."

Did that mean he intended them to spend the evening together?

She was in so much turmoil she didn't argue with him.

After she removed her coat, she took the package she'd purchased at the drugstore to the bathroom. She wasn't sure what she hoped for. She wanted a baby. She wanted Garrett's baby. But did she want one like this?

The test was easy to use. Afterward she waited in the bathroom. There was no point going out there and pacing along with him. When she checked her watch and examined the stick, she saw the negative sign.

Sagging against the counter, she didn't know if she was relieved or sad. She knew what Garrett would be, though.

Tossing everything into the waste can, she returned to the living room. He was sitting on the sofa, staring into the fire. And she couldn't even imagine what he was thinking.

When his eyes found hers expectantly, she told him, "I'm not pregnant."

No expression crossed his face, but he patted the sofa next to him. "Come and sit." It was more than a request but less than an order.

He looked so sexy…and dangerous in the black T-shirt and jeans, his hair ruffled from the wind, his face all strong lines that added up to determination and resolution, and maybe something gentler. He was sitting forward on the sofa cushion. She sat further back and rested her head against the top of the sofa.

"Are you relieved?"

She closed her eyes. "Part of me is. The other part really wants to be a mother."

"Is that why you forgot about birth control?"

Her eyes popped open and she sat up. "What do you mean?"

"Maybe you wanted to get pregnant, and I was a means to an end."

Anger rose so fast her cheeks got hot. "No. That wasn't my intention. Why did *you* forget about it? Did you want to be a father?"

"Of course not. For those few minutes my sex drive overrode my common sense."

She could have been insulted by that. But this was Garrett. He wouldn't admit if feelings had taken over. "Maybe our subconscious is telling us something in both of our cases."

"Don't try to analyze me, Gwen. You won't get far."

She wasn't so sure about that. Garrett had a hard shell, that was true. But there were cracks in it that she could sometimes peer through.

The fire was releasing outdoor wood scents, filling the room with warmth and a soft crackle.

"Why did you really come over tonight?" she asked softly.

"I told you I wanted to find out if you were pregnant."

"You don't think I would have called you if I was?"

His shoulders tensed and he ran his hands through his hair. "You might have. You might not have."

"You know I would have. So, why tonight?"

Now he looked frustrated and almost angry. "What do you want from me, Gwen?"

"I want to know what you're feeling, what's going on in your head."

His gray eyes were stormy as he finally admitted, "All right. I couldn't stay away from you. I didn't like the way the other night…ended."

Love for Garrett filled her heart. But she told him honestly what she'd been feeling after they'd made love. "I felt as if you didn't want me here. I felt as if I were something you *had* to deal with, not *wanted* to deal with."

He leaned closer to her now and stroked her cheek. "And you don't stay where you're not wanted?"

"Not anymore."

"I want you, Gwen. I've been fighting it, but I *do* want you."

His lips covered hers possessively...with a demand she knew wouldn't end with a kiss. As intoxicating waves of desire washed over her, she knew she didn't *want* it to end with a kiss. Maybe her dream wasn't an impossibility. Wouldn't his feelings for her grow the longer they were together? The fact that he'd been fighting the bonds growing between them was a sign his feelings for her were growing deeper...stronger.

She'd always thought about the future, always tried to plan ahead, because she'd discovered early she could only depend on herself. Maybe it was time to stop planning ahead and just think about now.

When the telephone rang they were both startled by it. Garrett swore and she murmured, "It might be Tiffany."

Reaching for the phone on the end table, Garrett picked up the receiver. "Maxwell," he said in a tempered voice that Gwen knew might be for Tiffany's benefit.

After a few seconds of listening, he said, "I'll call you right back."

To Gwen, he explained, "I have to handle this call. I'll go up to my office. You *will* be here when I come down?"

Curious, but knowing her questions would have to wait, she nodded.

Garrett mounted the stairs to his office and shut the door.

Fifteen minutes later Garrett's office door opened and he returned to the living room.

"Who was it?" she asked.

"It was work-related."

"And you can't tell me about it?"

"I can't tell you about it."

Could she accept this aspect of Garrett? That there might always be secrecy? If she trusted him, the secrecy wouldn't matter. Then she remembered Mark and all the things he hadn't told her—his doubts…his fears…his unreadiness to get married. She thought about her father, why he drank and how he never explained to her what was going on inside of him. Would there come a time when there were too many secrets…too many feelings *not* shared?

Garrett must have seen her inner battle because he came to her, surrounded her with his arms and leaned back to look into her eyes. "I got the government contract."

"And they call on a Friday night?"

"Government types don't take off on weekends…or sleep," he confided with a wry smile. Then he got serious again. "I can't discuss the particulars with anyone, Gwen. That's just the way it is."

This time she *could* read something on Garrett's face—hope that she could accept what he'd told her… hope that they could be together in spite of his lifestyle.

Making a decision, she stroked his jaw. "I'd rather you'd kiss me than tell me about your work."

When he kissed her, she let the moment take over.

She let "now" guide her. That's just the way it had to be with Garrett.

This time, she was going to go with the flow…and maybe she'd find her bliss.

Garrett's hands were on Gwen. Gwen's hands were on Garrett. Their clothes were definitely in the way.

The fire threw both light and dark shadows. At one moment Gwen could see Garrett's face clearly. At another, he angled his head and the darkness in the room concealed the lines on his face and any emotion in his eyes. As she had before, Gwen waited for flashes of light when she could see hunger and desire. Then she could convince herself there was even more.

As with everything else about him, Garrett's desire was focused and intense. When he touched her, she felt such exquisite yearnings, she couldn't breathe.

He didn't ask permission when he grabbed hold of the hem of her top and lifted it over her head. "Do you know how hard it was for me to stay away from you these past two weeks?"

"Why did you?" she asked, wondering how she could get him out of his clothes as fast as he could rid her of hers.

"Because I wanted to give us both some time, not only to find out about the pregnancy, but to let you think about what you wanted."

"I want *you*," she breathed as he took her breasts in his hands and bent his head to kiss them.

She meant it in a much broader sense than what they were doing now, and she hoped she wasn't deluding herself into thinking it could happen. Mark hadn't told her he wasn't ready for marriage, at least not for marriage with her. Garrett had made his terms plain—live in the moment…seize the day. Marriage was an institution he didn't want to be chained up in.

She'd asked herself over and over again if she could be satisfied with that…satisfied with loving Garrett but maybe not entwining their lives with vows and a gold band. Even though he didn't think marriage was in the cards, she hoped he wasn't dismissing children altogether. She hoped even without marriage she might still become a mother…and give Garrett the gift of being a dad.

Garrett's finger was wickedly erotic as it encircled her nipple, teased and taunted.

When she moaned, he laughed. "Your knees weak yet?" he asked with male satisfaction.

"I feel as if I'm melting in your hands."

"You can't melt yet. We've only just begun."

The melody of the old song played like a hopeful anthem in her head as she found new resolve and reached out to tug his shirt from his jeans.

Breaking away, he tore it off himself and tossed it to the floor. As her hands stroked up his sides in teasing exploration, he bent, his forehead resting against hers.

"The condoms are in the bedroom." His voice was low, husky and filled with need.

"What about the fire?"

"It'll keep. I'll take care of it afterward."

Afterward.

Tonight…afterward…she wouldn't have regrets. Tonight…afterward…she'd hold Garrett and he'd hold her until morning. Tonight…afterward…she'd show Garrett that intimacy and vulnerability went hand in hand, and he didn't have to shy away from either.

When Gwen was an adolescent and her father rambled in a drunken stupor, the house needed to be cleaned and supper needed to be cooked, and she just wanted to be turned into somebody else who had a different life, she'd woven fairy tales. Well, *one* fairy tale about a strong, tall super heroic man, scooping her up out of the life she knew and carrying her off to a better one with him. That reality had gotten trampled by men and women's changing roles, by adolescent boys who weren't the superhero type, by a reality that compromised wishes. But that day when she'd spotted Garrett in his shed, and he'd turned his gray eyes on her, that fairy tale had arisen from the ashes, and she hadn't even realized it.

As if fulfilling a dream she'd almost forgotten, Garrett stepped away momentarily and scooped her up into his arms. Did she trust him to carry her? Could she depend on him not to let her fall in *any* sense of the word?

He seemed to read those questions in her eyes. "This is going to be good, Gwen. *So* good."

"I know it will," she murmured, and hung on to him as he carried her down the hall to the master bedroom.

When Garrett set her beside his gigantic bed, she barely noticed the Navajo blanket on the wall, the lodgepole pine bedroom suite, the navy-and-red quilt that felt thick and soft as her hand brushed against it. Garrett was her focus, and every beat of her heart made her more aware of him. Her feelings for him shouldn't shut out the rest of the world, should they? Her feelings for him shouldn't make her forget about past hurts, shouldn't make her see life anew, shouldn't urge her to reach for a dream she'd tucked away.

Should they?

While he reached around her to unclasp her bra, she wrapped her fingers around his biceps, stopping him.

"What?" he asked, looking concerned, as if she was going to stop everything here and now.

"I want this to last."

"Nothing lasts, Gwen. Absolutely nothing. You know that as well as I do."

Yes, she did, but still… "You don't want tomorrow and tomorrow and tomorrow?"

"I want tonight. Be here with me now."

She knew what he meant. She had trouble living in the present. She liked to plan and analyze and project. All of that made her feel as if life were more than random, as if she had some control.

"Tell me what you're afraid of," he prompted gently.

She couldn't. She couldn't tell him she was afraid he'd leave. She was afraid he'd get tired of her and move on. She was afraid his connections to his ex-wife might not be severed. She was afraid he'd keep himself hidden and she'd never really know him…never really know she could trust him. As he'd said, men didn't like to discuss.

For once, though, choosing the moment over the future, she wasn't going to spoil tonight with talk of her fears. Running her hands over his hot skin and up his shoulders, she raised herself on tiptoe and teased his lips with her tongue.

Groaning, he crushed her against him, her breasts pressed against his chest, his arousal snug against the V of her thighs.

"We can't do it like this," she breathed against his lips with a smile.

"Then let's get rid of these damn clothes," he said, but he didn't move to do it.

"You feel good," she whispered against his lips.

"You feel better than good," he muttered against hers.

When he rocked against her, she felt like a lit firecracker ready to explode. When he rubbed against her again, she climaxed. Just like that. It took her by surprise. For a moment she stiffened in his arms as the nerve-tingling sensations danced through her body.

"Oh, Garrett." She clutched him harder and he pressed into her deeper until she was weak against him.

As she opened her eyes, he was right there studying her.

"It shouldn't have happened yet," she murmured. "I mean, I don't even have my clothes off. I wanted to wait for you."

Laughing, he swung her up onto the bed. Then he stripped her, piece by piece, until she lay naked and he was looking down at her as if he couldn't wait to gobble her up.

Gwen soon discovered that Garrett was an active partner who didn't want her to lie passive, who wanted her to reach out and touch, kiss, lick, just as he did. He seemed to have an unending supply of erotic kisses, teasing touches and experimental nibbles that soon sent her to the edge of orgasm again. Almost playful with her, they rolled over several times in his big bed. She loved the feel of his long, hard body pressed down on hers, his coarse hair rubbing against her soft skin, his lips kissing a line from her temple to her neck. When they switched positions, he caressed her bottom and the backs of her thighs.

Suddenly, he brought her into a sitting position so he could caress her breasts and watch her face.

"You just want to see me blush," she teased.

"I want to see more than that. I want to see the passion start. I want to see it go so high you can't wait to have me inside you." His thumb stroked her secret nub and she moaned. "That's it," he said. "Give in to it, Gwen."

"I did. I have. I'm—"

"You're ready," he growled, "and so am I." Reaching over to the nightstand he picked up a packet lying there. "Do you want to put it on or should I?"

"That depends. How much can you take?" she asked coyly.

"As much as you know how to give."

That was a challenge if she ever heard one. After she took the packet from his hand, she tore it open and joked, "Does this glow in the dark?"

"No. But I don't think you'll have any trouble finding me."

No, she certainly wouldn't.

She rolled the condom onto him…touching, caressing, kissing. As she did, his whole body tensed and she smiled. "How're we doing?" she asked. "We're only halfway."

"*We're* doing just fine."

Leaning down to him, Gwen let her hair brush his groin as she finished rolling on the condom. Then she rubbed her cheek through the hair below his navel and kissed right above it.

"Okay," he groaned. "I think the foreplay's over."

"You can't take a few more hours of this?"

"*This* from the woman who climaxed before I had her clothes off."

A few seconds later he'd reached for her and rolled her onto her back. She gazed up at him, loving him so much it hurt. How had this happened so fast? How had he pulled the rope and raised the curtain on what could be? She had to stop questioning and just be grateful. She had to start living in the moment…with Garrett.

He had her arms pinned slightly but now she raised them and scraped her nails over his chest.

Closing his eyes for a moment, he finally opened them again and smiled. "You are so…"

"So?" she asked with a little laugh.

"So natural. So damn sexy I can hardly stand it."

"Then what are you waiting for?"

"I'm not waiting. I'm…prolonging. But I think we've both had enough of anticipation and we can always do this again." With that pronouncement he raised his lower body then urged her, "Bend your knees."

She no sooner had when he eased into her, slowly filling her, healing the emptiness she'd known all her life. It was miraculously gone and she couldn't blink away her tears. When had she last cried from sheer joy?

Although his eyes were glazed with desire, his hair

damp from their prolonged foreplay and restraint, he went still. "What's the matter, Gwen? Am I hurting you?"

"No," she replied quickly. "Anything but. It just feels so wonderful. I just love you being inside of me…"

She couldn't finish and he seemed to understand. Pulling him back to the moment, she contracted around him, stroked his back and finally murmured, "Don't stop."

The expression on his face told her he'd finally lost control. When he thrust into her more powerfully, she moved with him. As he headed toward satisfaction, she accepted every thrust, felt herself swirling toward erotic release, much different than she'd known a short while before. Every single one of her muscles tensed and trembled as Garrett joined with her again and again. She felt as if she were coming undone. The sensations were glorious, terrifying, extraordinary, and she cried out Garrett's name.

"Let go, Gwen. Go with it. Come with me."

She gasped as the orgasm overtook her…as it chased the trembling from her body, leaving in its wake fiery frissons of pleasure. The first wave of them hadn't ceased when a second orgasm shook her. As it did, Garrett stilled, shuddered, rocked into her again, then collapsed on top of her.

She could feel his heart racing just as hers was. A few moments later he raised his head and shifted to his side, separating them. She hated that feeling of separateness, as if they'd been wrenched apart from the most beautiful union she had ever known.

Did he feel that, too?

When she looked over at him, she didn't know what to expect. After all, this was Garrett—Mr. Inscrutable.

Reaching out, he trailed his fingers down her cheek, over the tracks of her tears. "I'm speechless," he admitted.

She loved the feel of his sweat-slicked body close to hers. She loved the closeness she felt, sharing the intimacy of his bedroom. She loved their scents mingling in that raw, after-sex way. "I hope you're speechless because it's the best sex you ever had."

Keeping a light tone now was probably best. If she told him she loved him, she had the feeling he'd go all remote...that he'd put time and distance and space between them.

"It was the best sex I ever had."

Coming from any other man, that could be a line. Coming from Garrett, she knew he was serious.

"I'll be right back," he assured her, then slid out of bed and went to the bathroom. A few minutes later, he returned and gathered her into his arms. Grabbing the sheet, he threw it over them.

His stomach growled and she laughed. "Hungry?" she asked.

"Yeah. But that and the fire can wait. I just want to hold you for a few minutes."

And she wanted to hold him. Maybe men's and women's needs weren't so very different after all.

Chapter Twelve

When the phone next to Garrett's bed rang, Gwen needed a few moments to come awake. By the time she did, his arms weren't around her anymore.

He was sitting on the edge of the bed, alert, his expression intent as he listened. "Hold on. I'll get her. She's right here. It's okay, Tiffany."

The sound of Tiffany's name had Gwen sitting straight up. Panic began beating against her chest as she took the phone from Garrett. "Tiffany? What's wrong?" Glancing at the clock she saw it was 2:00 a.m.

"Amy won't stop crying and I don't know what to do. I've never seen her like this. She's been fussing since nine o'clock and I'm afraid I'm doing something wrong, or she's sick. I didn't want to call you." There were tears in Tiffany's voice and Gwen wondered how long she'd waited before making this call.

"Honey, calm down. Take a breath. Does she have a fever?"

"I used that ear thermometer we got but it's hard to tell. She's so hot from crying."

"What did the thermometer say?"

"It said 98.6 but I don't know if I'm reading it right."

"Tell her I'll bring you home," Garrett said close to her ear. "We'll be there in fifteen minutes."

Fifteen minutes later, Garrett insisted on going into the house with Gwen. She didn't protest. She knew people didn't often go out of their way for each other. She, Kylie and Shaye always had. But their small circle had been pretty much a closed one, and Gwen hadn't known unselfish giving from many others. Now Garrett didn't seem perturbed or put out or even upset about his lack of sleep as she enfolded a crying Tiffany into her arms along with the baby.

Tiffany finally pulled away, looking embarrassed, especially when she glanced at Garrett. "I've laid her on her stomach, I've laid her on her back, I've rocked her and walked her and played music. I don't know what else to do."

When Gwen took the baby into her arms, she could feel Amy's little legs coming up to her stomach. She suspected the infant was simply having a colicky night. When she used the ear thermometer herself, Amy did not have a temperature. But she was riled up, crying and in distress. Gwen suspected this had started with some sort of stomach upset and snowballed.

"I can call Dr. Pinelli's service—" Gwen began.

"Why don't we take her for a ride?" Garrett suggested.

Gwen and Tiffany both stared at him.

He addressed Tiffany. "Didn't you tell me she always falls asleep in the car?"

"Yes, but—"

"It's worth a shot, isn't it?" He had to almost shout to be heard above Amy's crying.

"It's worth a shot," Gwen agreed. "And, if it doesn't work, I'll call the pediatrician."

Five minutes later they were all in Garrett's SUV, Amy in the car seat he'd purchased for days he'd be chauffeuring Tiffany and Amy home to Gwen's. Tiffany sat next to Amy in the back. The baby's cries seemed to fill the whole world as Garrett backed out of the driveway and drove up the street. He was controlled, calm, seemingly unperturbed by the whole ordeal. How many men would go to these lengths to help a teenager who worked for them?

The streets were practically deserted, and at first, Amy's cries still rent the air. Then there was a subtle change. They became not quite as high-pitched, not quite as sustained. By the time they'd traveled five miles on the road to Cody the baby was hiccuping and would finally take the pacifier Tiffany offered.

"Oh my gosh!" she said almost with awe. "It's working. Mr. Maxwell, you're a genius!"

He laughed and to Gwen it sounded a little wry. She had no doubt he was thinking about his own baby, maybe how fatherhood would have affected him. Maybe how it might have changed his life.

A half hour later, when they returned to Gwen's, she was afraid Amy might start crying again as soon as the car stopped. But the infant stayed asleep and Gwen knew that was from sheer exhaustion.

She said to Tiffany, "Shaye had one of those swings for Timmy. I told her I'd let her know if we needed it. If Amy likes motion, that might quiet her when she's fussy."

"I've got to save up for a car," Tiffany decided with a huge yawn. "Then you two wouldn't have to drag me around."

After Tiffany carried Amy into the house, she headed toward her room. But before she left the living room she turned to face them. "I'm so sorry I had to call tonight. I didn't want to bother you. I didn't want you to think I couldn't handle Amy on my own. But I knew I had to do what was best for her."

"Yes, you did. You did the right thing," Gwen assured her. "Now go on, get some sleep while you can."

With a nod, Tiffany yawned again, then ambled down the hall.

Garrett made no move toward Gwen, and she didn't quite know what to do now, either. She remembered the safety and excitement and happiness she'd felt as he'd held her in his huge bed.

His brows drew together as he asked rhetorically, "We can't sleep together with Tiffany here, can we? You're going to tell me you want to set an example for her."

"We can snuggle on the couch," she suggested lightly, knowing he was thinking about all of the disadvantages being involved with her would bring. She wasn't a free spirit anymore. She had responsibilities that entailed more than her own life. Before they'd found Tiffany, he hadn't wanted to get involved. Now there were even more reasons, very practical ones, why his life would get very complicated if he did.

"I want more than snuggling on the couch," he growled.

She could see that hunger in his eyes again—the hunger that had driven their foreplay…the hunger that had made him reach for her, and her for him…the hunger that would have led them to make love again if Tiffany hadn't called.

"I know my life is complicated. I know this isn't what you expected."

In a stride he was close to her, towering over her, the lines around his eyes deep from lack of sleep. "We don't usually get what we expect. You've rattled my life, Gwen, and that's damned uncomfortable. But I want a repeat of the first part of tonight. Somehow, we'll carve out time, if you want it, too."

"I want it, too."

When he kissed her, she wanted to tug him back into her bedroom, forget about responsibilities and go with the moment again. But their next moment would have to wait.

As he leaned away, she knew he didn't want to leave any more than she wanted him to leave. "Tell Tiffany she doesn't have to come in today," he said gruffly. "She needs sleep. I know you don't want to leave her in the evenings after being at work all day."

"She's going to a workshop tomorrow night for new mothers."

He jumped on that. "How long does it last?"

"Six to nine. I can drop her off and then drive out to your place."

"Sounds good to me."

Three hours with Garrett tomorrow night didn't sound like nearly enough. Would he tire of them trying to match their schedules, of considering a child and a young mother in the mix?

As his arms enfolded her and he kissed her again, she hung on to her love for him and hoped, in time, he'd come to feel a like love for her. If he did, then meshing their lives could be easier than either of them realized.

But love was the key. Without it, they'd fall apart. He'd leave…

Giving her heart and soul in their kiss, she didn't think about the future, only the here and now.

When Garrett awakened at 10:00 a.m. the sun was basting the room with its early November warmth. He'd gotten home around 4:00 a.m., fallen into bed and sunk into sleep. Now he spotted the empty condom wrapper on his nightstand, saw the impression of Gwen's head in the pillow next to him. He listened to the absolute silence, broken only by the wind against the window.

He'd been alone ever since his divorce. The silence had never bothered him before. Today it did.

Because the sound of Gwen's laughter filled his house when she was here? Because her presence warmed it in a way furniture and a fire never could?

With no doubt, she was the most responsive woman he'd ever met…and the most frustrating. But her dry humor, her give-as-good-as-she-got attitude, her giving nature had sucker-punched him. Now he didn't know if he *wanted* to recover.

Critically, he thought about his baggage—a job that had turned him cynical, a divorce that had made him feel like a failure. He thought about vows he and Cheryl hadn't lived up to and about the baby they'd both lost.

He remembered his lunch with Cheryl in D.C. Why had she felt the need to tell him about her pregnancy? For closure? To really find out what he thought? Why now after all these years?

For advice?

He hoped she'd wanted closure and finally had it. He did. Cheryl's life didn't concern him. If she married or didn't marry, that was none of his business.

Now he was going to move forward with Gwen...and hope they wouldn't tear each other's hearts in two.

The outside light from Garrett's shed illuminated him as he chopped wood. Gwen watched him from the kitchen window, admiring the precise athletic way he moved. Days were getting shorter now in November. Thanksgiving wasn't far away.

Would they celebrate it together? She wanted so much to share the holidays with Garrett...all of them. She could envision them sitting around a table with Tiffany and Amy and her dad. Maybe even Kylie would come. Was it a wayward dream? The hope was so brand new she was almost afraid to embrace it.

The ring of the kitchen phone jarred the peaceful stillness.

For a moment she thought about picking it up. After all, she felt at home here now. For the past few days they'd managed a bit of time alone each day. Last night

Tiffany had visited a young single mother she'd met at her parenting workshop. Gwen and Garrett had spent almost the entire evening in bed.

She loved lying with Garrett, having him hold her. She wished they could do it every night. She wished...

The phone rang a second, third and then fourth time. She listened to the message in case it was important, in case it was something that had to do with his work. He'd told her he had to go to D.C. again next week.

Garrett's "Leave a message and I'll get back to you as soon as I can," preceded a beep. Then a woman's voice began, "Garrett, it's Cheryl."

Everything inside of Gwen came instantly to attention. His ex-wife. If their lunch had been a final parting of ways, why was she calling?

"It was good to see you in D.C. It's hard to believe The Trellis is still there, the way restaurants come and go. Anyway, I thought about everything we talked about and—" She hesitated. "I'm not going to marry Dennis now. We're going to wait until after the new year and see what happens. Thanks for being honest with me. Give me a call when you get back to D.C. before Thanksgiving. Maybe we can get together again."

When Cheryl hung up, Gwen felt as if she'd been kicked in the stomach.

Were Garrett and Cheryl over? If she was postponing her wedding, if he'd told her he'd be in D.C. again...

Mark had backed out of *their* wedding. Because he hadn't loved her enough? Because he hadn't been ready for a family? Or because he'd realized he'd loved his ex-girlfriend?

Garrett and Mark weren't anything alike.

A cynical voice inside her head whispered, "But they're both *men.*"

She paced from the kitchen counter to the breakfast nook and back again. Had Garrett only taken his ex-wife to lunch? Had they gone to her place? Or back to his hotel room?

Damn it. Had she been an absolute idiot again? Had she let some supposed mystical connection between her and Garrett, which was probably a combination of pure lust, hormones and pheromones, blind her into dreaming?

Had she been living in a fool's paradise for the past few days—thinking about the holidays spent with Garrett, planning what she might give him as a Christmas present, debating about whether or not she should tell him that she loved him?

The sound of the ax splitting wood stopped. Her heart was pounding too hard, and she reminded herself to stay calm. For a moment, she almost panicked and thought about calling Kylie or Shaye to get their advice.

But Kylie and Shaye weren't in her shoes. Shaye had never had to face the possibility of Dylan loving someone else. With everything Kylie had gone through with Alex, *she* might understand what Gwen was facing.

And just what was she facing? The possibility that Garrett still loved his ex-wife? That they could possibly get back together? That he'd never intended to give his heart to Gwen in the first place? That sex was simply sex for him and nothing more?

All the advice in the world wouldn't tell her what

was in Garrett's heart. She had to see that and hear that for herself.

When the back door opened, she didn't move. She almost felt paralyzed. She guessed that's what fear and the dashing of hope did. She'd thought she'd hit the bottom of an emotional well the day Mark had left her at the altar. But she knew now she hadn't loved Mark as deeply as she loved Garrett. She knew now that whether Garrett realized it or not, he'd become the linchpin of her world. She envisioned them growing so close he'd want to have kids. Maybe even get married someday. In her fantasy she'd seen them growing old together, sitting on his deck in rocking chairs, holding each other's hands and hearts and lives.

At this moment, she understood why her father had used alcohol to numb the pain.

The November wind carried an icy bite as it swept into the kitchen and swirled around Gwen's heart. The pages of the calendar on the wall fluttered, and Gwen realized Garrett had opened the door, and then gone back out to fetch the wood. Only a few ticks of the clock sounded, then there he was in his navy flannel shirt, insulated vest, arms full of logs for the fireplace.

"Can you get the door?" he asked as he strode through the kitchen to the living room.

She wasn't sure what made her move then, whether it was his request, the cold air blowing down from the mountain, the surety that she had to know the truth right now. Kylie had given Alex the benefit of the doubt over and over again because she hadn't wanted to believe the worst. Gwen had accepted Mark's silences and his halfhearted passion because she hadn't known she deserved better.

But she'd thought she'd found better with Garrett. She'd thought she'd found lasting.

When she closed the door, she shut coming-of-winter out, and all of her worries in. In the living room she could hear Garrett stacking the logs in their cubbyhole.

She could stay silent. She didn't have to tell him about the message. She could hold on to the illusion that they were a couple…at least for tonight.

However, she'd never been very good at deluding herself, and she couldn't live with herself if she did.

Two table lamps glowed in the living room. She watched as Garrett took kindling from a fireside basket and positioned it on the grate. After he lit the dry wood, he positioned a log on it, then closed the fire screen. When he straightened and unzipped his vest, she knew she had to start somehow. She knew she had to get the answers to her many questions.

"You got a call while you were outside."

When she didn't say more he quirked a brow. "Did you answer it or let the machine take it?"

"I let the machine take it."

He was looking at her quizzically now. "I guess it wasn't search and rescue, or you would have come and gotten me."

"No, it wasn't search and rescue. It was your ex-wife. You should probably listen to it."

Although the light in the room hadn't dimmed, his face seemed shadowed now. Crossing to the kitchen, he stopped when he reached her and hesitated a moment. But then he went to the counter and pressed the play button.

The message that had shaken Gwen's world played again.

As Cheryl's phone message faded away, the echoes of it still seemed to vibrate in the kitchen.

"Tell me what you're thinking," he demanded.

It was the demand that frustrated her. As if she had done something wrong. "I'm thinking that I don't know what to think. She's postponing her wedding. She knows you're returning to D.C. What's going on?"

"Nothing is going on."

"After the two of you had lunch, did she go back to your hotel room with you?" She couldn't hurt any more than she did right now, so she might as well keep going.

His eyes and voice grew steely hard. "You don't trust me."

"How can I when I hear a message like that? What am I supposed to think?"

"You're supposed to think I had some personal business to take care of and that's what I did…in a restaurant. I've never given you any reason to doubt me."

"Yes, you have. I doubt you because I just don't know you. You're guarded, Garrett. I never know what you're really thinking or feeling. You kept quiet about my dad's interest in search-and-rescue work. You didn't tell me you were considering taking him up with you. You won't tell me about your work…it can't all be classified."

Obviously frustrated, he shook his head. "This is exactly why I haven't been involved seriously since my divorce. What do you want from me, Gwen? Total disclosure as to how I've spent every minute of my day? Access to every thought in my head?"

What she wanted was his love. And now she realized she would probably never have that. So instead, she said, "I want you to tell me what's going on with your ex-wife. I want the truth."

"All right, then, here it is. I hadn't been in touch with Cheryl for years. Suddenly one day, she leaves a message on my machine. We played phone tag, and when I went to D.C. I decided to try to call her while I was there. When I did, she asked if I'd have time for lunch. We met at The Trellis, a place we used to go to. When I first laid eyes on her—I got a shock because she was pregnant."

Gwen's mouth went dry, but somehow she managed to ask, "No reminiscing for old times' sake?"

Still in that even-this-isn't-any-of-your-business voice he answered, "Sure, we reminisced. But I think she wanted advice. Apparently she got involved with this man because she wanted a child. Now she realizes a baby isn't a good reason to marry. Now she realizes they don't really know each other very well, and marriage could be a mistake. Or maybe she just wanted me to analyze her situation and put that into words."

Softly Gwen suggested, "Maybe she realized what she had with you was much more special than what she has with him."

Garrett's hand slashed through the tension, dismissing her suggestion. "We screwed up what we had. I did. She did. That's history. Apparently she called today to give me an update."

"Maybe she wants to get close again."

"I don't think so. I think she was just glad for a listening ear. But whatever her motives, they don't concern me anymore. Her life decisions have nothing to do with me now. We hurt each other badly, and with that kind of history I'm not even sure we can still be friends. The point is, Gwen, I saw Cheryl for about an hour when I went to D.C. The rest of the time I was in meetings. And if you don't learn how to trust, you're going to be alone for the rest of your life."

She took that verbal blow on the chin but wouldn't let it keep her down. "And what about you, Garrett? If you want to be a recluse that's fine. But if you want something serious, if you want something good, you can't just open up your life halfway. You can't control every thought and every emotion. You have to let yourself *feel*. You can't expect a woman to be a mind reader. You can't hold back and then get angry when a woman wants more."

"We're talking about *you*, Gwen. *You* want more. Maybe I don't have more to give."

"And maybe you're afraid to give. Maybe you don't trust any more than I do."

"You think I don't trust you?"

"I think if you did we wouldn't be having this conversation."

When he was silent she knew he was going into his remote mode. She knew the discussion had ended. "You said if I don't trust anyone I'll be alone the rest of my life. Being alone might be better than not knowing a man's level of commitment and always wondering and worrying how soon he'll want to leave."

"Not all men leave," he growled.

"There are lots of different ways to leave, Garrett. Closing down is one of them. I should have known better than to expect—" The tears that flooded her eyes closed her throat. She wouldn't stand here and cry in front of him. She wouldn't let him see how much she hurt. She wouldn't let him know that loving him had cost her the last vestige of hope that two people could love unconditionally and become one.

"I'd better go," she mumbled as she went to get her coat from the chair in the breakfast nook.

Garrett still remained silent. He didn't move toward her, and he didn't tell her to stay.

As she left him, she prayed he'd call her name. But he didn't. She knew they were over.

Chapter Thirteen

At the edge of town on Saturday morning Gwen filled her minivan with gas, thinking about what she still had to do for Kylie's baby shower the next day. When she heard the buzz of an airplane, she looked up into the gray sky and spotted a small plane. As she examined it closer, she saw navy and white against the gray sky, spotted the identifying number on the tail and knew it was Garrett's. He must have just taken off from the airport because he was climbing higher.

A search-and-rescue mission? A business trip? A private jaunt? The weather forecast predicted snow for later. Maybe he was going away for longer than just the day.

Or maybe a child needed him and he had no choice.

The sight of the plane put another tear in her heart. It had been three days since she had seen him. Three days of silence. Three days of questioning herself and what she wanted and what she could give. She wanted to be with him. She owed him an apology. But giving her trust was a huge issue. He'd never told her how he felt about her. She didn't know if pure physical need drove him when they were together, or if there was something that went as deep as her love for him.

As she drove into the mountains to stop at the shack of a financially strapped mother-to-be who only had a woodstove for heat and no transportation when her husband was on the road trucking, snow began to fall. These home health visits were as much about emotional support as physical care. She hadn't been able to fit these two into her schedule this week, and she'd decided they couldn't wait. The health of their unborn babies was at stake.

Gwen answered Nancy's questions, gave her a book on breast-feeding and went over emergency childbirth, in case the woman was alone when the process started. She encouraged her to go into town and stay with a friend if she could, but Nancy just shrugged and said she'd think about it. Gwen knew there was nothing else she could do.

After another visit to a rural mom with three children who lived in a trailer and was recently divorced, Gwen saw the snow was heavier now. Her van was covered with about an inch, and as she brushed it from the side windows she worried about Garrett. What were conditions like for him? Was he in any danger?

Beginning her descent down the mountain, Gwen realized how careful she'd have to be. The light layer of snow made the roadway slick. As she rounded a curve, she felt the van wheels slip and antilock brakes take hold. Proceeding at a crawl, her hands tight on the wheel, she peered ahead into snow that was swirling now. On the same side of town as the airport, Gwen didn't think twice about heading for Garrett's hangar rather than driving into town.

She veered off the drive to the airport, taking a snowier road that circled around the main building to the private hangars. When she pulled into the parking area beside Garrett's, she was surprised to see her dad's car. She was sure that was his car. The blue Toyota had a bumper sticker that read, I BRAKE FOR GRIZZLIES.

The giant doors where the plane went in and out were closed, she supposed to keep out the snow. Going to the side door, she opened it and went inside.

Garrett's hangar, like the others for small planes that were connected to it, was a large, mostly empty space. In one corner there were two stuffed chairs that looked like renegades from a thrift store. Between them sat a table with a lamp and a radio. Magazines were stacked on top of a small refrigerator. There were also two folding chairs and a large toolbox against another wall. Garrett's mechanic, Dave Johnson, was pacing, a cell phone at his ear, something that looked like a walkie-talkie in his other hand.

She waited until he snapped the phone shut, his expression much too sober.

"I thought I saw Garrett take off this morning. I was hoping he was back."

"Not yet. He's on his way."

"In this storm?"

"He didn't have a lot of choice. The front moved in faster than anyone expected. Your dad spotted the kid, though, right before it did and the ground search-and-rescue team moved in to pick him up."

"My dad's with Garrett?"

"Yeah. Garrett tried to talk him out of going. He knew the weather was going to turn, he just didn't know when. Apparently your dad called him when he heard on the news that a teenager had a fight with his dad and had taken off into the Bighorns. He'd been gone a couple of hours before one of his friends got worried and told the parents."

"Are you in touch with them? Garrett and Dad, I mean?"

"Sure am."

"So can you tell me what's happening?"

"They're in a snowstorm in a small plane. Garrett's an expert pilot and he's using his instruments. He should be checking in again with me shortly. All we can do is wait."

Gwen wasn't good at waiting. Never had been. Never would be. Her mind raced with probabilities and possibilities. While Dave called someone on his cell phone, she turned back time. She thought about Mark, meeting him at the hospital, dating him, becoming engaged to him. It had been a very practical and convenient relationship. Safe, too, in its way. No fireworks. No extreme highs or lows. It had been predictable…until Mark hadn't shown up to marry her. He had been the smart one.

Would anything have been different if she'd given him more? If she'd really become vulnerable and put her heart completely on the line? Had he returned to an old love because the newer one hadn't worked? Because the woman before Gwen had stolen his heart and kept it?

It didn't matter now, because Gwen had met Garrett, and any idea she'd had about love being convenient or practical had evaporated when she gazed into his gray eyes. She'd felt the burn of desire from the moment she'd laid eyes on him and he'd laid eyes on her. Their first kiss had defined fireworks in a new way. Not only that, but they complemented each other. He treated her as an equal and she felt like his partner, when they were searching for Tiffany and when they were in bed together.

Everything that had happened between the two of them played over and over in her mind. The baggage she carried had made her doubt him. She knew he was a man of integrity. She knew he was a protector. She knew he was honest.

How could she have doubted him?

That was easy. She loved him more than she'd ever loved anyone. She loved him so high and deep and wide, the extent of it had made her afraid...afraid she was loving alone. Afraid he couldn't accept her and her flaws. Afraid of giving her heart freely and unconditionally, without asking for his in return.

She had to tell him. She had to ask for his forgiveness. She had to give him her trust along with her love.

* * *

Garrett's headset enabled him to communicate with Russ, as well as radio Dave. Glancing at the older man next to him, Garrett saw no fear on his face. Maybe he had too much confidence in his pilot. Conditions were deteriorating.

Garrett spoke to Dave, knowing Russ could hear him, knowing Russ knew the danger almost as well as he did. "The wind's starting to gust. Visibility's diminishing. ETA fifteen to twenty minutes. Over."

"The runway's drifting," Dave told him. "Over."

"I'll keep that in mind. Over."

"One more thing," Dave said. "There's a lady here waiting for you, so don't screw up the landing. Over."

"Gwen's there?"

"Roger that," Dave acknowledged.

After Garrett absorbed that information, he ended the call.

Russ remained silent as the snow swirled and the strobe lights on the wings cut through it, freeze-framing the flakes. If Garrett had to rely on his own senses, rather than instruments, he'd think they were suspended in time, going nowhere, with no up or down…no left or right…just a white cocoon where they could float forever.

He'd been floating the past few years. He just hadn't known it. He thought he'd been living. But he hadn't been. He'd realized that the moment Gwen stood in his shed. She'd taught him that life was about more than going through the motions. It was about more than working and searching for lost children. In the course of his search today he'd realized he could find every lost child in the world, but if he didn't forgive himself for Cheryl's miscarriage, he'd never be happy.

It was his own fault Gwen doubted him. Everything she'd said the other night had been true. He'd kept his heart locked. The past few days, he'd been functioning on autopilot, missing her, trying to untangle his thoughts and his life. Now as he peered out into the white-gray world, one fact was clear. He loved Gwen Langworthy. He loved her and they were going to make a life together. If she would accept his apology. If she would forgive his denial of feelings he'd been afraid to confront. He had to unlock his heart...for her...for them. If he really opened up to her and told her how much she meant to him, maybe then she could learn to trust him.

"It's something up here, isn't it?" Russ asked.

"Something dangerous right now," he answered wryly.

"Not if you know what you're doing. And *you* know what you're doing. I wouldn't be up here with you if I thought differently."

After a few moments passed, Garrett said, "Tell me something. If someone hurts Gwen, is she likely to forgive him?"

"You mean like that guy who didn't show up for what was supposed to be the most important day of her life?"

"Do you think she forgave him?"

"Yeah, I think she did. Actually she took the blame on herself just like she did with me. Every time she gets hurt she thinks *she's* the one at fault. Her real parents left her. What was wrong with her that they did? Her mom walked out. What did she do to cause that? And then there was me. I turned to a bottle instead of caring for her. She thought she could have been a better daughter."

"We talked about that and I told her she's not to blame for any of it. There's nothing wrong with *her.*"

"Of course there's not. But I think she needs someone with no ax to grind to show her that. Not just tell her. She needs someone who will put her first. She needs someone who can be loyal and true. Are you up to the job?"

"She told you—"

"She didn't tell me a thing. But I'm her dad, and I'm sober now."

Garrett's gaze made the standard T-scan of instruments.

"Once we get these wheels on the ground you don't have to worry about somebody being loyal and true to Gwen for the rest of her life."

"I don't know whether you want it or not, but you've got my blessing."

Garrett could feel the older man's kind gaze on him. Just because Russ Langworthy was on his side didn't mean Gwen would welcome him with open arms. But somehow he'd prove to her he wasn't the SOB she thought he was. Somehow he'd prove to her that he loved her.

Peering up into the sky from the wide-open hangar doors, trying to see through the snow, Gwen heard the buzz of an engine. Closing her eyes, she prayed Garrett would have angels under his wings. He might be an expert pilot, but in these conditions…

In spite of the weather, she stepped outside. She heard

Dave call her name, but she couldn't stay still…couldn't stay inside…couldn't not see Garrett fly in.

What was Garrett thinking right now? What was her dad thinking? Two of the people she most cared about in the whole world were—

The next moment she could make out the speck of color against the snow. The plane's engine droned louder, the aircraft became visible and then it was coming down.

She didn't know anything about runways, but examining this one she saw the gusts of wind lifting snow, depositing it in mounds. Uneven mounds. Some places the surface was almost bare. Others had maybe two to three inches of snow. It looked bumpy and uneven, and she found herself holding her breath as snow collected in her hair, on her coat then swirled away in the force of the wind.

Unable to take her eyes off the plane, she thought it looked as if it was coming in okay. It really did.

Forcing herself to breathe, she watched until it ducked lower and lower onto the runway, watched as the angle changed and the nose slightly went up before the landing gear touched down hard. Very hard. Then it all happened fast. The plane seemed to twist sideways, slide and one wing tipped to the ground. After spinning around 180 degrees, it finally righted itself.

She took off onto the runway even though Dave called her name again.

The doors on the plane opened. First her dad got out, and then Garrett. Relief overwhelmed her. They were in one piece. They were fine. Everything was going to be okay.

She kept repeating the words like a mantra as she ran toward them. All she wanted to do was throw herself into Garrett's arms. But she knew he might not want that. She knew he might not want *her.*

So she went to her dad first and gave him a giant hug.

Snowflakes landed on her lashes as he pulled away and asked gruffly, "What in the hell are you doing out here?"

"I had to make sure you were okay. I had to make sure Garrett—"

Her dad grinned at her. "Go get him, baby."

Were her dad's eyes twinkling? Misting over? No, it was just the snow.

Men in down jackets were attending to the plane. Garrett was speaking to one of them. Then he focused his attention on her.

She thought about going back to the hangar and waiting for him, but she couldn't stand waiting another second more. As he strode toward her, his leather jacket repelling the white flakes but his hair collecting them, she froze in sudden panic. She'd made a spectacle of herself running out here.

Garrett was just going to have to deal with it, and what she felt for him, because she couldn't keep it in any longer.

"Let's go inside the hangar," he said, his voice gruff.

"Not yet. I want to apologize. I never should have doubted you. I'm sorry, Garrett. It's just that I love you so much. I know you probably don't want to hear that, but—"

His hands came up to her cheeks and cupped them. His skin was warm in spite of the temperature outside.

"This is not the place to do this," he decided with a crooked smile. "I wanted to wow you with soft music, flowers, a little humble pie."

The wind buffeted them and his arms went around her to pull her tight and close. "I'm sorry, too. I'm sorry I didn't understand how my lunch with Cheryl looked to you. I tried to convince myself it wasn't important. I tried to convince myself it had nothing to do with you and me. But it did. It helped me put the past in the past. I know I've had my heart closed to you most of the time. But still, somehow, you've managed to slip inside. I love you, Gwen. I understand now that you didn't trust me because you didn't know how I felt. You didn't know that no woman in the world is right for me but you. You didn't know that I was finally learning the meaning of the word compromise. You didn't know that I need you more than I need work or flying. Or even—" he grinned at her, "—chocolate cream pie."

Her tears were hot on her cheeks, and he ducked his head to hers and kissed them away.

"I believe you're the one woman who can accept the challenge of the life I want to lead," he murmured. "And if you can't, we'll do something about it. I love you, Gwen. Will you marry me?"

"I love you, Garrett, just the way you are. I know your work is important. I know searching for children is important. I know you can't promise me you won't fly in a snowstorm again. But I want you to promise me that you won't take unnecessary chances, and you'll remember how much I love you, no matter what you're doing."

"It's a deal," he promised, his lips close to hers.

Then he kissed her, standing in the midst of a snowstorm, allowing the Wyoming wind to buffet them but not affect them...because they were warm and safe, surrounded by each other's love.

When he lifted his head, he scooped her up into his arms and began striding toward the hangar.

"What are you doing?" she laughed.

"I'm taking you someplace where it's warmer. And then I'm going to take you home with me, make long, slow love to you and propose properly."

"Naked...on one knee?" she teased.

He laughed, and the sound of it heated her as much as the strength of his arms.

When they reached the hangar Dave looked on quizzically, but Garrett ignored him as he set her down.

"I want to marry you today. But if you want a wedding with all the trimmings, if you want all your friends there, I can wait. Just not too long."

"Let me talk to Shaye and Kylie and Tiffany and we'll see how soon we can pull it together."

Lacing his hands in her hair, Garrett kissed her again. The snow, the hangar, the soft sound of her dad's words as she heard him say, "Thatta boy," all faded away as her kiss promised Garrett her trust and her love. His promised her a fulfilling future together, absolute commitment and unconditional acceptance of who she was and who she wanted to be.

This time after he broke away he looked serious. "Call Tiffany and tell her our good news. Tell her I landed safely and in a couple of hours we'll pick up dinner at The Silver Dollar and bring it home."

"I have a commitment to her," Gwen said softly.

"I know you do. And so do I. We'll work it out."

She knew they would. Because she and Garrett belonged together…for the rest of their lives.

Garrett tested the latch on the stall door as Dylan poured feed into one of the bins at Saddle Ridge on Sunday afternoon. Looking over at Shaye's husband, Garrett realized a friendship had developed between him and Dylan this afternoon as they'd helped feed the cattle and now did odds and ends around the barn.

"Do you think it's safe to go to the house yet? My stomach's rumbling. Those casseroles Gwen baked for the shower smelled awfully good."

"So did the chocolate cake with coconut icing that Shaye brought along. What's the worst that could happen if we go in?"

"We'll get drawn into a discussion of the best diapers to use and which car seat is safest."

Dylan laughed. "That's not such a tough price to pay for good food."

"Shaye tells me you and Gwen are planning a simple wedding."

"It's starting out that way. I don't know how simple it'll be until we get finished with it. Gwen's going to call the minister tomorrow for an available date."

"Shaye and I got married a week after I came to my senses. She and Gwen and Kylie pulled it together fast.

We had a candlelight service in that old church over on Red Point Drive."

"How do you feel now about doing it so fast?"

"Shaye and I had no doubts. And we're still on our honeymoon." He added with a grin, "That is, when Timmy lets us *be* on a honeymoon."

Garrett nodded. "Gwen and I are sure about this, too. I don't know how Tiffany and Amy are going to play into it. Gwen and I talked about that last night. I told Gwen we could sell her house and add another room onto mine. We might need it eventually, anyway."

"Shaye and I want to give Timmy a brother or sister. But I think we're going to wait until he's out of diapers."

Garrett tried the latch on the stall one last time. "I don't know how Kylie's going to handle this place once her baby comes."

"She doesn't want to accept help," Dylan commented.

"I know. She's as stubborn as Gwen."

"And Shaye."

The two men exchanged a look that said they loved their women and wouldn't have them any other way.

Once inside the house Garrett realized the baby shower was still in full swing. Several women he didn't know were chatting. He noticed a little girl of about ten who hardly left Kylie's side.

Gwen was setting the casseroles she had reheated in the oven on the table. He slipped his arm around her waist and kissed her neck. "Hey there, beautiful. How much longer is this shindig going to last?"

"Just until everyone eats. Aren't you hungry?"

"Always. But more for you than the food."

When her cheeks reddened, he laughed. "We could sneak out to the barn."

"Yes, we could. Maybe when everyone's eating they won't notice."

He couldn't tell if she was completely serious or not. Yet that's what he liked about Gwen. She was game for almost anything. What he loved about Gwen was that she was game for *him*.

He nodded to the little girl beside Kylie. "Who's that?"

"Her name's Molly. When she took riding lessons, she got attached to Kylie. They both love animals. Her mom's the redhead on the folding chair by the window."

Garrett glanced at the woman briefly, at Dylan who had taken Timmy from his wife's arms, then at Tiffany who was cuddling Amy in an old rocker. "I know this might be a little soon to bring this up, but how do you feel about having kids?"

"I love the idea of having *your* kids."

Taking her hand, he winked at her, and as unobtrusively as possible led her around the edge of the party to the door. "We'll be back before they know we left."

Gwen laughed, slipped out the door with him and ran to the barn.

Life with Gwen was going to be an adventure, and Garrett was going to appreciate every moment of it.

Breathless, he took her into his arms when they reached the barn's side door. "I love you."

"I love you, too."

Garrett kept hold of Gwen's hand as he led her inside.

This was only the beginning, and no matter when they married, he was going to make the honeymoon last as long as he could.

At least for the next fifty years.

* * * * *

Don't miss EXPECTING HIS BROTHER'S BABY,
the next book in Karen Rose Smith's miniseries,
BABY BONDS—available
in September 2006
from Silhouette Special Edition.

Page-turning drama…

Exotic, glamorous locations…

Intense emotion and passionate seduction…

Sheikhs, princes and billionaire tycoons…

This summer, may we suggest:

**THE SHEIKH'S
DISOBEDIENT BRIDE**
by Jane Porter

On sale June.

**AT THE GREEK TYCOON'S
BIDDING**
by Cathy Williams

On sale July.

**THE ITALIAN MILLIONAIRE'S
VIRGIN WIFE**

On sale August.

With new titles to choose from every month,
discover a world of romance in our books written
by internationally bestselling authors.

HARLEQUIN® *Presents*

It's the ultimate in quality romance!

Available wherever Harlequin books are sold.

www.eHarlequin.com   HPGEN06

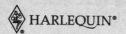

If you enjoyed what you just read,
then we've got an offer you can't resist!

Take 2 bestselling love stories FREE!

Plus get a FREE surprise gift!

Clip this page and mail it to Silhouette Reader Service™

IN U.S.A.	**IN CANADA**
3010 Walden Ave.	P.O. Box 609
P.O. Box 1867	Fort Erie, Ontario
Buffalo, N.Y. 14240-1867	L2A 5X3

YES! Please send me 2 free Silhouette Special Edition® novels and my free surprise gift. After receiving them, if I don't wish to receive anymore, I can return the shipping statement marked cancel. If I don't cancel, I will receive 6 brand-new novels every month, before they're available in stores! In the U.S.A., bill me at the bargain price of $4.24 plus 25¢ shipping and handling per book and applicable sales tax, if any*. In Canada, bill me at the bargain price of $4.99 plus 25¢ shipping and handling per book and applicable taxes**. That's the complete price and a savings of at least 10% off the cover prices—what a great deal! I understand that accepting the 2 free books and gift places me under no obligation ever to buy any books. I can always return a shipment and cancel at any time. Even if I never buy another book from Silhouette, the 2 free books and gift are mine to keep forever.

235 SDN DZ9D
335 SDN DZ9E

Name	(PLEASE PRINT)	
Address	Apt.#	
City	State/Prov.	Zip/Postal Code

Not valid to current Silhouette Special Edition® subscribers.

Want to try two free books from another series?
Call 1-800-873-8635 or visit www.morefreebooks.com.

* Terms and prices subject to change without notice. Sales tax applicable in N.Y.
** Canadian residents will be charged applicable provincial taxes and GST.
  All orders subject to approval. Offer limited to one per household.
  ® are registered trademarks owned and used by the trademark owner and or its licensee.

SPED04R   ©2004 Harlequin Enterprises Limited

Stability is highly overrated....

Dana Logan's world had always revolved around her children. Now they're all grown up and don't seem to need anything she's able to give them. Struggling to find her new identity, Dana realizes that it's about time for her to get "off her rocker" and begin a new life!

Off Her Rocker

by Jennifer Archer

Available August 2006
TheNextNovel.com

SILHOUETTE *Romance*

A family saga begins to unravel
when the doors to the Bella Lucia
Restaurant Empire are opened...

The Brides of Bella Lucia

*A family torn apart by secrets,
reunited by marriage*

AUGUST 2006

COMING HOME TO THE COWBOY
by Patricia Thayer

Find out what happens to Rebecca Valentine when
her relationship with a millionaire cowboy and single
dad moves from professional to personal.

SEPTEMBER 2006

The Valentine family saga continues in

HARLEQUIN® *Romance*

with **THE REBEL PRINCE** by Raye Morgan

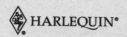

HARLEQUIN®

American ROMANCE®

American Beauties

SORORITY SISTERS, FRIENDS FOR LIFE

Michele Dunaway

THE MARRIAGE CAMPAIGN

Campaign fund-raiser Lisa Meyer has worked
hard to be her own boss and will let nothing—
especially romance—interfere with her success.
To Mark Smith, Lisa is the perfect candidate for
him to spend his life with. But if she lets herself
fall for Mark, will she lose all she's worked for?
Or will she have a future that's more than
she's ever dreamed of?

On sale August 2006

Also watch for:

THE WEDDING SECRET
On sale December 2006

NINE MONTHS NOTICE
On sale April 2007

Available wherever Harlequin books are sold.

www.eHarlequin.com

COMING NEXT MONTH